The Cul-de-Sac

R. L. YOUNG

R. L. YOUNG

This story is a work of fiction. All of the characters, organizations, and events portrayed in this story are either products of the author's imagination or are used fictitiously.

ISBN: 0692141510
ISBN-13: 978-0692141519

To E and A; may you stay forever young.

ONE

The night before last a storm tore up a poplar tree and deposited it right on top of Leroy McGuff's dog kennel. Today I watched from across the cul-de-sac while Leroy watered the rosebush he'd planted where the kennel used to be. He already had dozens of the thorny, bloomy plants, lined up in an unnatural parade across his otherwise scrappy half acre of front yard. From my paused stance I thought I could smell the sulfurous hose water all the way from the bottom of my driveway. As usual, McGuff's beer belly led him through a sort of slow-motion march as he made his way along the bushes, a cigarette dangling loosely from his lips. I blinked at the scene. What the fuck happened to the dogs?

He started to turn and I quickly redirected my gaze to the mailbox, busying myself with the extrication of junk letters so he wouldn't be tempted to return my ogling. Eyes to gravel, I readjusted the pile of mail under my arm and headed back up my driveway. I neglected to note the brightly decorated Patricia Murgatroyd as she emerged from the house next door. When she wasn't talking she was an astoundingly silent person.

"JOHNNY! Yoo-hoo!" she trumpeted. With her gossip-detecting third eye she'd sensed me fifty yards away. I'd moved into the subdivision three months ago. I liked the big lots, and the houses were well back from the road. The dips and hills and uncommonly high number of trees increased the illusion of breathing space. Despite this, my privacy had become rather compromised of late. I mostly blamed the dead-end nature of the street. And Patricia Murgatroyd.

I smiled, my hand over my forehead to visor against the evening sun rays streaming from behind her.

"Would you believe," she gasped, motoring toward me through the grass, "the deer haven't got my strawberries yet? I was gonna make you a cobbler, dear, but I'm afraid I used them all for a batch of daiquiris instead. Would you like some? Strawberry daiquiri I mean? I can bring it over, I know how you prefer *your* deck. And I'll bring glasses too, I have some I don't think you've seen, they're from Spain, you know." She took a breath. "That *man*!" she spat, looking behind me at Leroy McGuff's waterworks. "What is he up to now? It's a wonder she lets him out of the house looking like that. Besides which, it's indecent to use flowers that way."

"Water them...?" I queried, raising my eyeglasses to massage a temple.

"Sell them, dear. He's in cahoots with that shady florist fellow down the road. The two of them have some sort of racket going on—drug stuff, you know. I'm sure of it." She paused, heaving a breath, and emanating a faint odor of stale rum and staler perfume. "I guess they can't all be as charming as you, Mr. Jepko. Daiquiris then? I'll see you in five," she beamed and turned tail, a svelte sixty-year-old, power-walking back to her yard. Nobody ambushed like Patricia Murgatroyd.

I circled my small house and followed the stone path around to the back, jogging up two steps to the elevated wooden deck. I deposited my mail on a wrought iron patio table before loosening my tie. Gray dust puffed skyward as I juggled charcoal from a bag into a grill in the corner. The muggy West Virginia heat lingered like an unwanted party guest. I reached up to plug in the string lights that hung crisscross from the rafters as the sun headed for the horizon. The wooden walls of the deck were three and a half feet high, leading up to support posts and open air that I'd chosen not to screen in. I thought it might feel too much like a cage.

I slid the unlocked glass door of my house open to let a shoddy calico cat blast out. In her wake I ducked inside to get an ice bucket and a couple steaks. The living room was full of paper and distinctly lacking in furniture. I navigated a short path to the kitchen, brushing past piles of blueprints, notes, sketches, and periodicals. The kitchen itself was bright and open, its normalcy serenely mocking my makeshift file room.

When I came back out, Patricia was already on the deck. Her flame-dyed pixie cut bobbed up and down as she rocked in a coil-spring chair. Two foil-wrapped corn cobs had appeared by the grill. A large glass pitcher filled with pinkish-red liquid and crushed ice sat on the latticed table. Patricia faced outwards to the thick woods beyond my backyard. She'd elevated her legs to a footstool, and her light green linen pants billowed in the breeze. I flicked on the amp inside the door and the tiny speakers above us began to whine jazz.

"Johnny," she said, closing purple-shadowed eyes, "if I were thirty years younger…"

"I am unworthy, madam," I protested idly, setting her sweating daiquiri pitcher into the confines of my ice bucket. Without looking she offered me a pre-poured cocktail goblet, and nearly drove it into my midsection. I sidestepped and grabbed it. Taking a sip, I nearly choked. I wondered vaguely if the deer had passed on her strawberries because they had not, in fact, been ripe. Patricia seemed to snap out of her momentary peace, or possibly stupor, as I stoked the charcoal.

"Just too nice of you to do steaks, dear—I'd never dream of asking, you know. Did you see the glass? I gave you the one with the *Sagrada Familia* on it," she pronounced theatrically. "I knew you'd like the architecture. It's a giant gothic church in Barcelona, you know. They've been working on it for a century and it's still not done: can you believe? My Rex would have really loved that one. He loved churches, you know...the buildings. Didn't care much for God."

I raised an eyebrow. Stepping back, I held my cocktail glass up to the dying sunlight to examine the etching. Rex Murgatroyd had died of a brain aneurysm at forty, leaving his precocious widow a small fortune and an overwhelming desire to travel. She'd spent the next decade never being at home. She'd managed to hit almost every tourist shop in the world, ridding them of one, or sometimes two selections of glassware. Then she'd spent the most recent decade drinking from all of them. These days, her only traveling involved flitting around local social circles, where she was considered something of a celebrity by sheer force of personality and liquor tolerance. I had inferred from many of her stories that Rex had been a drinker, too.

"Oh, get 'em! YOU GET 'EM!" she shrieked suddenly, bouncing in her seat like a rabid twenty-something at a Mountaineers game. Her drink sloshed around her glass as if it were trying to escape.

I peered out in the twilight to determine the source of her fervor. It was the calico cat, streaking by in hot pursuit of a smallish rabbit. They zigzagged out of sight as fast as they'd appeared.

"She got a shrew the other day, the darling," Patricia pointed out. "But shrews don't eat my vegetables. Those fucking rabbits eat my vegetables." She took a pinkie-raised sip of daiquiri.

I tested the heat of the grill with a hovering palm. Satisfied, I laid the steaks in the middle, and rolled the corn to the peripheries.

"What in the world, Johnny?" Patricia asked as I turned back around. Bored by my quietude, and loose in her definition of privacy, she had helped herself to my stack of mail. She held a particular item forward that had been lodged between credit card offers.

I frowned, leaning in for a better look.

"John...I think this is a blackmail note," she uttered with incredulity.

I tugged the letter from her hand.

"Last chance, Mr. Meers," it began almost comically, addressing my other next door neighbor. It proceeded to spell out a monetary demand of $20,000 as payment to avoid police exposure for unspecified "crimes committed." There was even a drop-off location at a nearby public park and a deadline of next Thursday. The note was made of cut-and-paste magazine letters like I'd seen in the movies. It reminded me of a twisted grade school craft project.

Patricia Murgatroyd and I stared at each other, mouths slightly agape. Above us, the speakers were playing a piano arpeggio. The grill snapped with a hissing drip of steak juice.

We burst out in laughter.

"Honestly, now, nobody blackmails anymore! This can't be real! Is this some sort of silly joke you're pulling, Johnny? You know, whistleblowing is the trendy thing to do these days. That Edward Snowden, he was kind of cute, too, I always thought. And twenty grand! Well that's not even enough to buy a decent car, you know—"

"Patricia," I said, forcing a pause. "Why was this in my mailbox?"

The letter was a single page, had no envelope, and was free of any telltale marks that it had passed through the hands of the postal service. It had been placed, not mailed.

"Well I suppose it's a mistake, dear. You're 105 Talon Creek Road, he's 115."

"One of his friends, maybe, pulling a prank, got his address confused...because they didn't already know where he lived?" I asked skeptically.

"I'm sure," she smiled at me, taking a big gulp of daiquiri. "Or they got the names confused, dear. Committed any atrocities lately?"

I gave her a glance and ignored her. "Do you know Mr. Meers?" I asked.

"Dillon Meers. Yes, I mean, sort of. I've only met him a few times. And he's lived here for years. He actually," she flipped a hand out to inspect her lavender-lacquered nails. "He's an odd one. He had a wife, you know, when he first moved in. Darby. Poor thing shot herself last year. Can you believe! Very uncommon for a woman to do it that way, you know. We're poisoners. Or drowners. Don't like to make a mess, or what have you." Her eyes narrowed slightly as she said the last, but then quickly softened as she continued. "It was all very sad. I know the girl's mother. And to think he hasn't moved. Still there in the house it happened in. And they didn't have kids, you know. It's all very tragic, really. Apparently he just came home to find her like that, can you believe? My Rex died naturally, of course, but even then I couldn't stand that big empty house all by myself, I moved here not even a month later." Her eyes wandered skyward as if she were seeing through the shingled roof of the deck.

I had listened to her brief account with my eyes to the woods, but now I turned back and picked up the blackmail note again. "Does someone thinks he killed her?" I asked.

Patricia nearly choked and turned wide eyes towards me. "My gawd, Johnny, no! I mean...well I mean maybe someone does, but he certainly didn't. Darby Meers was always a sad little thing. The police were very sure, anyway. She'd taken one of his guns, alright, but the forensics and whatnot backed it all up completely. He had nothing to do with it, wasn't even around at the time. But everyone knows that. No, I don't think anyone would blame him at all. In fact, I'm a little surprised it's not Leroy McGuff's name on that letter," she huffed, "I know he's up to something with those damn roses."

"Either way, we should probably call the police," I said, and then, dropping it on the table, "...and probably stop touching it."

"Oh, let's! A mis-delivered blackmail note! Calling the police! How fun! Maybe we can insert ourselves into the investigation! Wouldn't Jessica be proud!" she bubbled, suddenly happy.

I grinned cautiously, utterly lost.

"Make sure they come out tonight, though, I want to be here when they investigate. They'll want to go talk to him, won't they? And us too—we found it! Oh gawd. You don't think they'd tell him we turned it in, do you?"

"I'm sure they'll come tonight," I said, "it's early yet."

"Good," she nodded, "because tomorrow is my spa day with the girls at the floatation center, you know, the salt bath soak, and the manicures, pedicures, ends up taking all day, really. And Sunday is Mahjong with the country club ladies, and besides, the university garden club wants me to speak at a brunch thing," she rolled her eyes.

I scratched at my chin stubble and leveled a gaze at her. "Well, let's certainly knock out the civic responsibilities before your groupies need you."

She stood, and poured herself more daiquiri. "Tonight will be fine. And just because my friends are younger and slightly enamored of me does not make them groupies, Johnny."

I tilted my head.

"They're much more like minions," she mumbled into her drink.

"You were never going to make me a strawberry cobbler, were you, Patricia." I said evenly.

She secured a hand on her hip, turning away from me. "Not really, dear. Well I mean I considered it, briefly, but you know, the strawberries just didn't seem ripe enough."

TWO

Three months ago I bade farewell to the suffocating offices of my downtown Charleston architecture firm and let my apartment lease expire. I moved to the suburbs, semi-forested and generously distanced from factory smoke. I started an at-home solo business, and commissioned the deck a month later. I'd designed it myself: a 600 square-foot framework of exposed wood in an outdoor sea of trees and wi-fi. It fit snugly against the side of my tiny a-frame house, which didn't particularly deserve it.

As offices went, I may have downgraded, but then again, walk-ins had plummeted to zero. Of course, it came with a mortgage I wasn't sure I could afford. Not to mention a nosy, independently wealthy neighbor primarily interested in procuring my company and drinking. But I guess I deserved Patricia. And contrary to popular belief, I thought people were their truest when drunk. When your inhibitions are smashed, you're too at-peace for self-censorship. She was always drunk, so I never felt misled.

"You want me to call them, or will you, dear?" she

was saying, "It's just so *odd*, you know. We have got to tell the police to keep us secret, like anonymous informants or whatever they call them on the TV. I guess it could all be a joke anyway. I mean this is such a nice neighborhood, I've never even heard of there being any crime here!"

She wasn't wrong. This was the kind of neighborhood where the vandals used sidewalk chalk. The moonshiners were a little farther out. I flipped the steaks.

"Another daiquiri?" She held up the pitcher.

"You know, Patricia," I shut my eyes. "We're about to, in all likelihood, be visited by the police."

She raised a finely manicured eyebrow at me and poured herself one instead. Her gaze suggesting that she felt sorry for me, and that I was petulant, and jealous, and that she knew something about the universe that I did not. I picked up my cell phone and dialed the county sheriff's office.

*   *   *

"You're bein' blackmailed?" the dispatcher drawled again.

"No! No. I received a letter. Well I didn't *receive* a letter, we found—"

Patricia, who had briefly wandered to the other edge of the deck, now sashayed up behind me. She twisted the cell phone out of my hand and held it up to her own ear.

"Holly? Honey is that you? It's Patricia Murgatroyd, dear, I'm over here in Elmcroft Subdivision at 105 Talon Creek. Yes, yes I know, he's my neighbor, Johnny Jepko. Oh, terrible, I know, he usually has the brains not to try. *Recklessly* attractive, though. HAHA. Yes! So, anyway dear, what happened is, we found a blackmail letter meant for Dillon Meers, the fellow next door, but it was in Johnny's mail, can you believe. They want twenty-k, apparently." She sniffed. "No kidding at all! I've never seen anything so bizarre in my life, and you know I've *travelled*, dear." She briefly held the phone away and sipped from her goblet. "Doesn't say at all what he's done. You mind sending down an officer or two just to check it out? 'Course we haven't told Mr. Meers. Didn't want to upset anyone. Can't imagine what he's been up to over there. Yes. Yes dear. Thank you so much. You tell Walter I said hi. Uh-huh. You too."

I towered over her as she returned the phone to my hand. I opened my mouth to speak but she set in before I could get a word out.

"Do you want to play a game of checkers til they get here, John? Or wait. Wait! Gin rummy. That's it. That's what we'll do, I've got a brand new deck of cards. Plus, life's always a little more interesting with gambling. And gin - ha! Alright, back in a snap dear!"

She'd started moving away long before the final rushed words reached her red, Machiavellian lips.

I finished up at the grill and dumped the food on two plates. I stared at the row of rhododendron that lined the driveway of Dillon Meers' house. The cedar siding was just visible through the smattering of trees that separated our properties. I pulled a little at the collar of my white button-down, and straightened my tie. I wore a tie because working from home was still working; because formality and ritual assuaged my guilt; because a girl I knew once had bought me almost all of my ties. She had said she'd thought of me every time she saw a geometric pattern.

An agitated wren bickered at the cat, who I could feel staring at me. I'd forgotten to feed her. She had come with the house, abandoned by previous owners and somewhat neurotic.

"You've got to feed that cat, Johnny," Patricia's

voice materialized, jarring me into awareness.

"Us first," I said, laying a plate in front of her. We sat dining as late-evening waves of sunshine oozed through the trees around us. I glanced around as I chewed, feeling guilty about abandoned my well-paying job. Once the cold weather hit, I'd have to get all my work done inside, which meant squeezing into the corner of the living room with the blueprint plotter. I'd barely gotten it into my house, and didn't relish moving it. The bedroom would be an option if I hadn't crammed the drafting table in there. I was second-guessing a drafting table; I was wondering if anything in any field would ever be done manually again, besides murder-for-hire and coal mining.

*   *   *

"Why are you wearing a tie?" the female deputy was asking me an hour later.

I had one arm crossed over the tie, supporting the other arm, which supported three fingers, which formed an annoyed pyramid on my forehead. I risked glancing up and cast about sideways for Patricia.

"Oh he always does, dear," she said, leaving the older detective to glide in for the rescue. "He works from home, you know, but still keeps it classy, huh! Really quite wonderful of him, I think, don't you? You know he's about your age, dear." Patricia winked at the deputy.

Detective Silas Giles had gruffly introduced himself fifteen minutes earlier; now he approached me again.

"Is it really a good idea to be parked in my driveway?" I asked, eyeing the cruiser sitting in plain sight beside my Tacoma. "If he—if Mr. Meers has committed some sort of crime worth blackmailing, I don't want him thinking we know about it. Or more importantly, told you all about it. Shouldn't you go ask him why he's receiving blackmail letters?"

The detective held the evidence bag containing the note in one hand. He'd kept his other hand loosely fisted above his holster since he'd arrived. Not in a nervous kind of way. Just professionally relaxed, from what I guessed was years of practice...preparing to shoot.

"But he didn't receive the letter, did he. You found this tonight?" he asked.

"Yeah. It was mixed up in my mail. I didn't notice it till I had it down here on the deck."

"And you think it was in your box by mistake," he said, his voice treading ambiguously between question and statement of fact. He had a well-trimmed mustache of graying hair and was almost as tall as me. He ran a thumb over the mustache now, waiting for me to say something.

"Well, yes. It's got his name on it." I gestured. "About the car..."

"Why did you say *letters*, plural?" Detective Giles continued.

I frowned. "Because it said 'last chance' or something. I assumed it wasn't the first."

"And...this is your mother's house?" he raised an eyebrow towards Patricia.

"No! No. She's not my mother, she lives over there, in 110. But she was *here*, when I found it. I mean, *she* found it." I sighed and closed my eyes.

"I see. If it comes to that, we'll explain to Mr. Meers that we interviewed his neighbors before him as standard procedure." The detective nodded slightly, and I got the distinct impression that I had bored him. "Could you send Ms. Murgatroyd back over?" he asked.

I bowed out of the way, sidling across the deck. I glanced at the cat that had taken cover indoors. She looked out at me through the glass door with what I could only interpret as a shit-eating grin.

"Patricia," I vaguely gestured, "Detective Giles would like to see you."

I considered for a minute the current state of entropy being visited upon my wooden fortress of calm.

"You know what," I announced loudly, "I might just go over there myself, see if he's home. His car's in the driveway. Give him a little heads up, you know."

I started striding towards Dillon Meer's property. I knew a little about how blackmail worked, myself.

"Sir. Sir!" The female deputy got in my face immediately, "Please stay on your property."

Detective Giles rolled his eyes and shuffled off the deck, nodding to Patricia. "We're going over there ourselves right now, Mr. Jepko, stay on your own property, please." He shoved the evidence bag to the deputy, and they loaded into the cruiser, twin doors slamming shut.

I grinned a little at my success. Patricia shot me a look of reproach.

"Well, pull up a chair, Johnny," she said, still half-frowning. "If we're lucky we can use that zoom lens on your fancy camera to see when he tries to escape."

After I'd retrieved my Canon from inside, we situated ourselves. The cops had already been in my driveway for several minutes. They were no doubt running social security numbers and scribbling notes about my inability to speak clearly. My feelings weren't hurt. I ranked verbal communication right up there with the ability to truss a Cornish game hen or win at chess—nice talents, but you could still make a living and get laid without either.

Patricia was clearly expecting some sort of spectacle to unfold, but I was busy regretting my behavior towards the police. They dutifully drove next door, shiny patrol car twinkling through trees. They pulled in next to Meers' shitty Mercury station wagon and the old green Jeep that never moved. Patricia poured herself the last of the daiquiri. The female deputy rang the doorbell.

Patricia focused my 250mm lens on my neighbor's kitchen window and studied the big LCD screen. A commercial jet took off from the airport two miles away and flew almost directly overhead. The noise drowned out the sound of the deputy pounding on Mr. Meers' front door. The deputy tried the doorbell again. Patricia put down the camera.

"Well he's not *in* there, Johnny." She pouted.

"His car's there," I stated just as pointlessly.

"I was watching the back door, too. He didn't make a run for it," she informed me, long nails rapping briefly on the table.

"These kinds of tragedies happen all the time," I told her. She looked a little as though the tragedy of her alcoholism was peeking through from under her sartorial rainbow today. "Is something wrong?" I asked.

"Oh don't mind me, Johnny. I just really want a cigarette. It's the humidity, I think. This whole blackmail business doesn't sit with me right. It's kind of unnatural, even if it is a joke. I feel like something bad is gonna happen."

"I didn't know you smoked," I said.

"I quit twenty years ago. Still suffering from nicotine withdrawal today. Don't let them tell you it goes away," she sipped her cocktail and waggled a finger at me. "You just have to replace it with booze and get really good at distracting yourself."

We watched the police pull out of Meers' driveway and disappear down the road. The sky had gotten truly dark. The leaves shuffled around us, splaying slick silver undersides that caught the reflection of the deck lights. A thunderstorm began spitting rain and thunder boomed around us. We scooted chairs away from the rails and I leaned inside the house, queuing up a symphonic film score on the deck speakers. I sat back down in a lounge chair. With bracelets clanging and pink heels stomping, Patricia Murgatroyd swept around my deck directing her orchestra of trees with a cocktail glass. The thunder and wind backed her up while I watched.

THREE

Six months ago my closest companion hadn't been a 60-year-old widow. She'd been a 26-year-old brunette. She had half-drawly speech and half-smiling lips. She had dark doe eyes and she didn't care for social media. She was fearless. She danced around my kitchen to classic rock with a paper-towel-rod microphone. She described our city as "the forgotten Charleston." If anyone even mentioned South Carolina she wrinkled up her nose as if they'd stolen something from her. She could truss up a Cornish game hen and she could beat anyone at chess. She melted me.

She told me once that two years before she met me she'd given up on ever finding me. I was late, and it was killing her. She said I was her greatest tragedy, and she used to shriek for me to leave with her nails dug in to make me stay. I never asked her for anything, because I was too busy drowning in our sin. And eventually, she left me. But I guess I never had her.

Today Patricia Murgatroyd was asking me about her. Which was mostly my fault. I didn't talk a lot, but Em was in my head unbidden most of the time and bits and hints of her leaked out in things I said. Patricia, savvy for all her hysterics, had begun to piece together a ghost.

"How'd you meet her?" Patricia started in with no context. She was hedging her bets on taking me by surprise. I hadn't seen Patricia for several days, and she'd just walked up out of nowhere. I sometimes didn't understand what she was up to during the week, social engagements notwithstanding.

"In a dream," I quipped, adjusting my glasses in annoyance. My afternoon client meeting had been cancelled and I'd been having it out with a small gang of carpenter bees when she approached. My deck was my most prized possession. It was the only thing about my house that I liked, that I had designed myself. And the bees were eating it, tunneling corruption in and spitting sawdust out. The sprays hadn't worked, the putty hadn't worked. I eyed the rafters, palming the handle of a badminton racket purchased for the sole purpose of entomological loss of life. I planned to take them out one by one.

As Patricia was asking me about Em a bee emerged from between rafter planks, coming into range. I leapt, wailing the racket in a violent arc. An anti-climactic ping sounded and the bug dropped dead to the wooden floor.

"Oh! We're in a little bit of a rage today, aren't we?" Patricia laughed, unconcerned by me or bees. "Good shot though! You play tennis?" She took a seat and slid me a glass of I-didn't-know-what. "That neighbor boy Jason Controy is on summer break and I'm having him do my weeding on Thursdays, now. You don't mind if I spy on him from here, do you dear?" She smiled at me. I think she was wearing purple lipstick.

"Help yourself," I sat, accepting the drink. It was a rum and coke. She was drunker than usual. I wanted to be drunk more than usual.

"You know, Johnny," she leaned back, long teal earrings bouncing off teal bloused shoulders. "I think that girl is cigarettes to you."

I knew what she meant and ignored her.

"They're fucking with the integrity of my deck." I pointed at the bee carcasses scattered about from my afternoon's efforts.

"It is a lovely deck, dear," she smiled, eyes trained to her garden next door. "He had better not be watering that rosemary. Jason! JASON!" She'd stood up and leaned her torso on the top rail of the side deck, holding her floppy sun hat with one hand while she waved about with the other. "JASON! IT RAINED YESTERDAY, SON! DON'T WATER THE ROSEMARY. YES. YES. THE SPIKY ONES. NO WATER!" She sighed loudly and retreated from the rail, collapsing back into her seat. "He's not an overachiever," she told me, "he thinks if he does extra I'll pay him more."

"Do you?" I asked.

"Of course I do," she pursed her purple lips and sucked in watered-down rum.

The cops pulled up next door moments later. I couldn't hear their tires on the gravel, because Patricia was drowning them out.

"WOULD YOU LOOK AT THAT!" She was beside herself. "They are HERE, AGAIN! Or there! What do you think happened? Did they never find him? That must be it. Oh, no! It's Thursday! Today was the day on the note, right? Are they escorting him there into the hand-off, you know, and then they step in like a sting operation? Oh my gawd, I wonder if we can ride-along? You know they do those ride-alongs on the TV, John!"

The calico cat had wandered up, and paused to hiss at me. I let the cat inside. "I don't know," I offered.

The next ten minutes seemed like ten hours, during which the cops theorized and waited for Dillon Meers, and Patricia theorized and waited for the cops. By the time Detective Giles plodded through the trees to my deck, I had finished the rum and coke and abandoned the insect war.

He allowed himself one questioning glance to the badminton racket, and one more to the cocktail glasses, before he spoke.

"Good afternoon, Mr. Jepko, Ms. Murgatroyd," he acknowledged, "have either of you seen Mr. Meers since we were here last week?"

"Oh my, no," Patricia said, "Have you, Johnny?" I shook my head. "We never really see him, Detective," she went on. "I mean, not more than what—once every couple months, maybe?" She looked to me, and I shrugged. "Yes. I mean Johnny here of course lives right next door, and I can't see his house from mine but I'm here a lot and I can't say I've seen the man's car even move but once a week. I think he is a very efficient shopper," she added.

Detective Giles blinked at this information.

"So when was the last time you actually saw him?" he pressed.

I looked at Patricia, and she looked at me.

"I see the wagon leave sometimes," I said, "but the last time I actually saw *him* was like a month ago, or more? He was checking his mail, and I was driving out to 7-11 or somewhere. I stopped and introduced myself, it was a couple weeks after I'd moved in."

"You know he doesn't shop there for his real groceries, Detective, but Johnny is very particular about his pop tarts," Patricia contributed, "he's convinced the blueberry ones have more filling than the others so he—" she stopped as I caught her hand and squeezed it, hard. She grasped it back and wobbled a little.

Detective Giles stared, nonplussed. "Okay," he said, "thank you both." He backed away immediately, pulling a cell phone out of his pocket. "I'm gonna need that search warrant," we could hear him saying, just before he stepped out of earshot.

"Well," I considered aloud, "that's either for us, because you're suspiciously wasted, or Dillon Meers, because he's a goddamn missing person."

"Either way," Patricia grinned, earrings slapping, "how *exciting!*"

*　　　*　　　*

Half an hour later two more police cars had pulled into Meers' driveway. Uniformed figures were bustling around like distant oversized ants foraging in the yard and woods. Unabashed, we stared at the activity. At first we traded theories, but then we trailed off into silence. Patricia tore herself away to go check up on Jason's weed-pulling progress. My thoughts stuck uncomfortably on Dillon Meers. I wondered what he'd felt when his wife died. I wondered if he'd lost his soul.

The terrifyingly loud alarm bark of a red fox suddenly rang out. My eyes darted immediately to the dry creek bed running the edge of our properties. Sure enough, I could see a police officer through the trees who had unknowingly approached the den. He'd fallen backwards in surprise when the vixen started screaming. I'd never heard the foxes make a fuss in the daytime before, but the sunlight didn't make the noises sound any less like murder. The cop was already struggling backwards, his embarrassed curses barely audible from my deck.

Patricia came back with slightly soiled zucchini, more rum, and wooden skewers. She waggled the latter at me suggestively.

"Fine," I said.

"They went all the way down to the fox den?" she asked, pouring me another drink and chuckling.

I pointed at the retreating officer. "Yep. Scared the shit outta him."

"Serves him right, messing with the poor darlings," she said. She liked every animal that wasn't a vegetarian.

In the next hour she'd gotten me half-crunk. The alcohol numbed my embarrassment, and I let her inside my house despite the evidence of hoarding disorder in the living room. I stood outside hacking vegetables into rounds, listening to a trumpeter meander around a solo on the speakers. From indoors Patricia accompanied my efforts with pithy whines about my lack of sharpened cutlery.

"Here," she finally came out with a mixing bowl full of raw meat. "Johnny, there's a drafting table in your bedroom," she added. The bowl contents were cold, and had from the smell of it been drenched in some sickly combination of Italian dressing and hot sauce. She offered me a handful of soaked skewers.

"What were you doing in my bedroom?" I asked.

"I insist on always using master bathrooms. Do you know what my favorite part about myself is, Johnny?" she asked, breaking up the soft squelches of hands in chicken slime.

"What?"

"Guess!" she stabbed a row of squash in my direction.

I sighed and made an attempt to smile. "Those sky-blue peepers?"

"Nope! Although I do have lovely eyes, don't I." She blinked mascara-laden lashes at me. "Guess again!"

"Impeccable sense of style?" I suggested, wondering

if orange pants were stylish.

"Ha! Aren't you a dear. But wrong! Guess again!"

"I don't know, Patricia." I punctured the last piece of chicken.

"My guilt!" she announced.

"Your...guilt?"

"Yes. It keeps my drinking in line, you see. I haven't driven drunk since 1978. Although I think I was more high than anything else," she amended. "It's God's punishment for not having kids, you know. Most parents just give their guilt away to their children. People like you and me are stuck with ours. Rex and I could never have children, you know, and he didn't want to adopt. Plus the business kept him so busy, I think it worked out alright."

I went in to wash the guilt and salmonella off my hands. When I came back out to put the kebabs on the grill she had grabbed a badminton racket as dance partner. She swayed around the deck to Stan Getz, like Em would have done.

"Dinner and a show!" Patricia announced when the food was ready. The cops had produced several German Shepherds, and the dogs quickly dragged their handlers around to the side of the house out of our view. Out of sight across the street, several other dogs apparently caught sight of the police shepherds and took up trading howls.

"Will you listen to that," I said, sipping my rum.

"What?" Patricia asked.

"Leroy McGuff's dogs. They *are* still over there."

"Well why wouldn't they be, Johnny!"

"That tree fell on his kennel..." I trailed off.

She shook her head at me and start wrapping up leftovers. I thought maybe she planned to feed the police, who appeared to be cordoning off an area in Meers' back yard with crime scene tape.

"Oh my gawd," Patricia said, noticing.

"We would have noticed a dead body, right. Buzzards, or something?" I stared.

She *tsked* at me. As far as I could tell no ambulances or coroners arrived. One by one the police rolled away, in sync with the disappearing sun.

"Kinda makes you want to wander over there..." I started innocently.

"Nonsense, Johnny. It's a police crime scene. We'll find out what it's all about soon enough."

I shook my head. Then I paused, and shook off my head-haze.

I nodded, then paused, and shook off my head-haze. "Are you...are you sober?" I eyed her, suddenly realizing that between my second rum and coke and the third she'd changed tacks. She'd been pouring me drinks and sparing herself. In fact, as I considered her tone, I was *sure* she was sober.

"I needed a break. I was feeling guilty," she informed me.

I bit forcefully into an ice cube. I could relate.

"C'mon, there's some light left," I sat my drink down and stepped off the deck. "Time for a little evening constitutional."

FOUR

Thirty years ago the first drops of asphalt splashed from the first dump-truck-fed paver, and since that day the Elmcroft Subdivision has had a road called Talon Creek. On the end of that road our cul-de-sac lay flattened out like a big toxic pancake. There was actually a creek by that name somewhere around here, but nobody had seen it for awhile. Apparently it had vacated when the houses moved in.

Four properties circled our particular street butt, abbreviated pie wedges in a jigsaw puzzle of one acre lots. Clockwise from the entryway was Dillon Meers, then myself, then Patricia, and then the McGuffs, then back to the entryway. Elmcroft Subdivision was proud to feature upper-middle class homes for overly ambitious young professionals, belatedly-settled married couples with half-matured kids, and wholly secured retirees. A little farther out, the hillbillies roamed willy-nilly on souped-up ATVs; a little farther in, the urbanites sweated furiously past rows of factories on eco-friendly bicycles. We were the seat of compromise and mediocrity, trading in our view of the stars for overbearing trees. Something about the West Virginian mountains kept this from looking like suburbs, but nobody was really fooled.

*   *   *

Patricia acquiesced to the stroll, and we headed down my driveway, arms linked. I needed support because I was drunk. She was just accustomed to being escorted.

"I should put my last name on my mailbox, I guess," I noted as we passed the plain black box that featured nothing but the smallish numbers of my address.

"Oh, I don't know, Johnny. People get targeted for burglary all the time, but in my experience people mistakenly receive blackmail notes very rarely."

"I don't like you sober," I let her know.

"Oh I know, dear. You wouldn't believe it, but I generally don't like people either. Look at that," she indicated, pulling me to a stop at the foot of Dillon Meers' driveway.

From this angle we could see clearly down the row of white rhododendron blooms to the area the police-tape encircled in the side yard. A generous run of tape was applied haphazardly to the front door.

"Oh my gawd," Patricia whispered fiercely.

"They really didn't find him," I contributed.

"But what *did* they find? Alright, Jepko. In we go," she adjusted her hold on my arm and yanked me forward in a manner that seemed to defy her being almost half my weight.

"Jesus, Patricia," I swung around to catch up. "What's your plan?"

"I know you have a pen light," she looked expectantly at me.

I gritted my teeth and handed her a small flashlight

from my pocket.

We wound around the vehicles and stepped off the gravel of his unpaved driveway into soft grass, creeping around to the side yard. Patricia shined the tiny beam of light in front of us but it barely shone in the evening light.

The shadows and damp smell in the air seemed to imply an upended grave, and the way Patricia clung to my arm I knew she thought so, too. On the ground, the reddish tone of unearthed clay was topside in short piles. Stretched unevenly from tree to tree, the block-lettered yellow tape surrounded unnaturally disturbed earth. Something had been forcibly uprooted.

"Oh!" Patricia said, loosening her grip on me and stepping closer. She held her hand over her mouth as she started laughing.

"What?!" I insisted.

"I think our neighbor was a bit of a gardener himself," she winked, and retrieved a leaf shred from the ground to show me.

"Oh goddammit," I wiped my brow and felt the tension leave my shoulders.

*   *   *

The police were surely confused when they found the marijuana plants in the back of Dillon Meers' house. We were. No way you could get the sunlight you needed for cannabis in these woods. Or that's what Patricia said. She said it wasn't a matter of criminality, it was a matter of horticulture, and I believed her. But it was supremely clever of Meers to put them on the other side of his house, opposite me, where he had no neighbor to spot them with a repurposed zoom lens. Though I doubt that had been on purpose.

"Plus," I pointed upwards to the dark blue glow of sky through tree silhouettes, "there's kind of a clearing here."

"That's horseshit," Patricia said, toeing the ground in a continuing fit of gardener jealousy. I gradually adjusted to our trespassing and looked around. I always thought of Em when I got drunk, and tonight was no different. After all, I'd moved here because of her. I didn't know how else to deal with losing her. "By no fault of your own," she'd claimed before she left. I always thought that was horseshit too.

We suddenly heard the sound of cachinnating teenagers through the trees. Flood lights flipped on over the top of a short rise. A cheap vehicle with expensive alterations rumbled to a stop down the road.

"Oh *no*," Patricia said. She sounded more upset than the situation merited. The teenagers certainly couldn't see us there in the dark shadows of Meers' house. As far as the world was concerned, this house was abandoned.

There was crime scene tape on Meers' side door, but none on the steps that led up to a small side deck. The deck was six feet or so up from ground level above the half-buried basement. Patricia insisted we climb up. We took the steps half-blind and situated ourselves on unfamiliar plastic chairs to get a better view of the kids. I looked nervously at the crime scene tape behind my shoulder, and Patricia seemed nervous. Neither of us looked at the kids.

"The Controys are out of town on some sort of second honeymoon," she said, glancing at me.

"Yes?" I waited for her to go on.

"Well you just, you know, you can't leave a boy alone like that, he's only seventeen!"

"You mean Jason has invited some friends over?" I asked.

"Friends! Johnny, that boy is spending the paycheck I gave him on a...party!" She pointed forlornly to a keg in the driveway. I chuckled.

"How's the guilt?" I asked.

"I'm going to go grab a drink. Want one?" She asked.

"Yeah," I agreed, confused as to whether alcohol was her problem or her salvation. I was too inebriated to figure it out and not sure I wanted to.

She took the flashlight and crunched her way back out to the road, and I turned my attention to the surreal activity next door.

A flurry of tiny black apparitions that I presumed were moths threw themselves endlessly at a couple of floodlights. The lights' motion-activation was frozen in the "on" position by constant movement. I recognized an outdoor beer pong tournament in the works. A long folding table materialized amidst a pack of t-shirts and jeans in the front lawn. It was quickly decorated with red plastic cup formations. I admired the foresight required to keep the mess mostly out-of-doors, but then again, it didn't look like a very spacious house. A small gang of miniskirts circled the slightly atilt, and surely illegal, keg in its tub on the sidelines. Every once in awhile the sound of an engine could be heard from Talon Creek road, followed by a group of figures trailing down the driveway. They entered the scene like anti-celebrities slouching along a black asphalt carpet, greeted with murmurs by unenthused peers.

Patricia returned with minimal gravel noise, betrayed only by the small beam of light that preceded her approach. She unloaded a Hawaiian-print tote bag right there on Dillon Meers' side deck. Out came a jumbo sealed bag of ice, and two glasses, and rum, and 6 little mini coke-bottles she'd overpaid for at God-knew-where. I loosened my tie, then tensed. A jet cruised overhead, pulsing lights like a traveling metronome in the dark sky. A couple of heads across the way looked up, but most kept their attention on the task at hand.

"You don't think the cops would come back tonight, right?" I asked.

"Didn't you go to Virginia Tech, dear?" Patricia asked, ignoring me to hand over a drink she'd assembled. She motioned to the muted beer pong.

"I am familiar with beer pong, yes. They weren't offering it as a major my year," I eyed her. "And I went to the University of Virginia. West Virginia doesn't have an architecture program, before you call me a traitor," I warned her.

"I have no feelings in regards to WVU, Johnny, I went to Georgia," she responded calmly.

"You did?" I blinked in the darkness.

"I did. I got my J.D. before you were even born, Jepko. Not many girls back then doing law, you know, but UGA was fairly quick, for a southern school, to let us in. I grew up in Savannah, born to be a debutante and all that. Well! I was made for more exotic things, as you might imagine. And then would you believe, I never practiced, and became a trophy wife anyway. Life really has a mind of its own, sometimes."

I stared at her in disbelief. "You're a fucking lawyer?"

"Go Dawgs!" she answered, bumping my glass with her own.

"Makes sense," I told her.

"What does?" she asked.

"That you're a transplant. Female sexagenarians, in my experience, are typically surrounded by grandchildren and small, yipping dogs, half-bedridden from sheer exhaustion and dying of lung disease."

"That's a horrible thing to say, Johnny," Patricia chided.

"Welcome to West Virginia."

We watched in silence for a few moments as the games began, lurking in the darkness of circus sidelines.

"You think this is really all about weed?" she asked suddenly, turning to look at me.

"Like, the blackmail? And him running? Seems a bit of an overaction—right? I don't know, how much trouble can you get into for growing weed? Or trespassing, I guess I should ask..."

"I never *practiced* law, Johnny, I don't know. But we're in West Virginia, not Colorado, so I would think a lot. Specially if he was selling it. It's really just so silly," she fumed, "I would at least have been able to respect a meth lab in the basement."

"Who d'you think knew he was growing it?"

"Oh, definitely Leroy McGuff," she said without pause.

"Oh, really."

"I bet he could almost see it from his front yard. He's directly across the street from here, you know. And he's always out there with his—his *roses*," she spat.

"Tell the truth, Pat. Did ole Leroy beat you in some kind of rose contest back in the day? The dogs piss on one of your azaleas, maybe? Wife snub you?"

"Don't be ridiculous, Johnny. It doesn't pay to be petty in this world."

"How about vengeful?"

"Jury's still out," she took a drink and fell silent.

She gestured to a teenager a few moments later. "He's my favorite."

I knew who she was talking about, because he was a head taller than any of the other kids, and looked like he would win. His shoulders were relaxed beneath a mahogany crew cut. He dribbled a ping pong ball once or twice on the edge of the table, letting it slap back up into his hand without looking down. His partner stood next to him in complete juxtaposition. Her tiny, blonde posture suggested utter impatience. They both seemed to be waiting on their opponents, who had become distracted across the table.

Jason, their host, though notably shy of six feet, was built like a wrestler. He appeared to be recruiting several brunettes on the sideline to be his personal cheerleaders. In his eagerness to procure a support system, he had failed to note that it was his turn to play. His partner, taller and slightly skeletal-looking, had his head bowed intently over a cell phone. The whole scene was one of vague chaos and distraction, everywhere the underaged were overexposed in hard light. Except for Patricia's would-be champion, and his angry little partner, the yard was full of chatter and movement. I watched the bravado jut of jaws and the betrayed demureness that erupted into loud laughs. There was a short line at the keg, and red cups multiplied like soul-beacons.

"Isn't that cute. They drink because they're happy," I chuckled. "We drink because we're not."

"Speak for yourself, Jepko. What'd you, throw in a Philosophy minor with that architectural degree of yours? You know, Rex majored in Philosophy. 'Course he always said it was because he was trying to destroy it from the inside. He went into business, in the end, you know. 'Murgatroyd Garden Supply - Grow Charleston!' Coal ash can do wonders for soil, did you know? Take advantage of your environment, that's what Rex always said." She laughed and softly clicked long nails on her glass. "Oh, okay. Here we go. Finally!" She leaned forward a little.

One of the teens had produced a Bluetooth speaker or something like it. Decades-old hip hop suddenly pounded into the night, the bass beat reaching us on Meers' deck. The party transformed, as if all the immature agitation had just been waiting on a soundtrack to relieve itself. The miniskirts started serpentining in rhythm and Jason seemed imbued with a newfound focus. He twirled a one-eighty and tossed a ping pong ball no one even realized he'd been holding like he was shooting a miniature basketball in slow motion. The yard erupted in cheers as it sunk with a splash in front of the Champion. The blonde snatched up the cup and chugged.

"Game *on*," Patricia said with no small amount of glee. I almost laughed, glancing at her. She was completely enrapt, chin to palm to elbow to delicately crossed legs. I turned back to the scene and watched the Champion and his partner line up next to one another.

"Oh shit," I laughed, "They're gonna run the table."

"What?!" Patricia tore her gaze away to give me a look.

The girl shot first, levelling an arm at the pyramid of cups across from her with an intensity the game didn't particularly merit. The Champion was already lining up as she shot, and seconds after her ball sunk, his came down in the cup next to it.

"Bring 'em back," I could see him say. A pouting Jason rolled the balls down the slimy table for a bonus turn.

Patricia looked at me desperately, and I explained what I remembered of the rules.

The Champion grabbed both balls and dipped them quickly in a water cup, then extended one out to the blonde like it was a gift. She finally looked at ease, wiping a hand on her jeans and accepting the tiny white sphere, shaking excess water off with a jerk and lining up. Then they sank both balls again.

Patricia slapped me in the arm without ungluing her eyes from the beer pong. "Oh my *GAWD* Johnny!" She hissed, "are they gonna get them back again?"

"Yep, I think," I said.

"How did you *know*?" She asked, finally turning to me.

"Well they haven't won yet," I said. "But they kinda had a look about them lining up together like that. You don't keep a girl like that around unless she can come through. Besides," I added, "I didn't learn beer pong at UVA. I learned it in Kanawha County."

"You're drunk and you guessed," she declared, dismissing me.

The two remaining cups on the opponent's side of the table were lined up one in front of the other, looking small. The winning partners abandoned their previous strategy. The Champion stepped well to one side so the blonde could stand in the exact center of their side of the table. She lined up unhurriedly, and shot. The aim was deadly but her angle was slightly off. The ping pong ball ricocheted off the back lip of the front cup and rattled back and forth several times. Then it sunk inside, accompanied by relieved sighs from the onlookers.

The Champion started to line up for the last cup and stopped. He dribbled the ball on the table in front of him once. The blonde stepped up and pulled his head down to her mouth. With her small hand grasped around his upper arm she balanced tip-toe to whisper something in his ear. His eyebrows rose slowly as her lips moved.

She promptly let go and stepped back, and the Champion turned and sunk the last cup before she'd even finished backing away. The crowd erupted.

"Hormones," Patricia muttered. "Those used to be fun."

"WHO'S GOT NEXT?!" the Champion roared to the crowd, and even we could hear him, then.

When Garth Brooks started proclaiming a scratchy

Friends in Low Places through the trees, Patricia calmly handed me one of two sets of earphones procured from the magic tote. It was attached to a splitter, which was attached to her cell phone. I fit the ear buds to my head. Eine kleine Nachtmusik piped in. I looked back up at the ongoing beer pong. Now I saw a perverse amalgamation of teenage gods, flung orbs, and sacrilegious ballet movements, according to the updated soundtrack. I started laughing.

"A debutante to the core," I complimented her.

"I don't know what you're talking about, Johnny," she sniffed. "I bought a keg of Natty Light today."

We two adults spent the evening silently entertained by teenagers in the dark, our sad maturity marked by our ability to watch fun without having any. To my credit, I made a clumsy pass at Patricia as she struggled to put me in bed after we'd stumbled back to my house in the dark. All it garnered me was the exploding raucous laughter of a sixty-year-old and a headache the next day that rendered me mostly immobile.

FIVE

Sometimes the possums and raccoons around here wander by houses in the daytime. They're not rabid, they're just not afraid anymore. They cut paths past dilapidated swing sets and trash cans. They advertise the wilderness, no matter what the occasional manicured yard may imply. The deer wander through by the dozens. They're impervious to the nearby airport noises and protected from hunting by the well-meaning homeowners associations. You can't put up a birdfeeder or you get creatures dangling off your eaves from everywhere. There was something grotesque and menacing about possums in sunlight. They weren't designed to be seen.

The cat must have spat out half a dead lizard on my kitchen floor the day before. I stepped on it barefoot first thing in the morning, unaware till I felt guts squish between my toes. I aimed my glasses down to see a weird little blue tail protruding from my footstep. While I ran bathwater over my toes, coffee in hand, I wondered if forests were the opposite of architecture. Out here all I designed was pretense; tiny boxes in vast forests, outdone on all sides by the constructs of mother nature. I probably should have stayed in the city, where mankind still had the upper hand. Em told me once I needed a pet or some plants or something in my apartment there, but I never saw the point. If she could see me now.

It was 9:30 Sunday morning and Patricia was already on my deck when I slid the glass open to step out. I cradled a laptop under my arm in hopes of a premature start on the work week. That was always my plan on Sunday mornings.

"Good morning, sunshine! I didn't want to wake you, dear, sorry if I startled you," she started up. "Look, I brought over some clematis and hyacinth vine clippings for these wonderful railings you have, but don't you worry, I'm going to plant them myself, I thought about doing containers so we could start them here on the inside but really it'll be so much better if we can get them in the ground. We'll just use a tomato cage or two to train them up to the height, or maybe you could design some sort of string system, I guess you are an architect, after all! And anyway I have to tell you what I saw on the news this morning on the TV!" She finally paused.

"Where are my eggs?" I asked numbly.

"No eggs this morning, Johnny, we're going into town, I'm craving pancakes and I'm all out of flour, can you believe, *flour*! You don't have any flour, do you? Doesn't matter, I've got my heart just set on brunch in town and I've got to pick up some things, you'll drive won't you? I just hate running errands alone and none of my girls get up this early on the weekends." She took a breath.

I looked at her, purse in hand, makeup fully applied, beaming wakeful sobriety at me.

"You want to go all the way into Charleston?"

"I'll pay for brunch," she lilted.

"I'll get my keys."

*   *   *

Twenty minutes later I almost got rear ended. Instead the driver behind me slammed his brakes and settled for a prolonged series of beeps, shoving a middle finger outside his window. I'd almost rolled my Tacoma to a full stop in the middle of the turnpike. In the distance a dozen girls in plain dresses and stark white bonnets stood around a patio table outside a coffee shop. They were giggling over iced lattes.

"What the fuck," I said to Patricia, who was urging me to speed up. "Seriously, though," I held out a hand like I was presenting the roadside irony to her on a platter.

"They're Mennonites, for Christ's sake, Johnny," she said sharply, "could we keep on?"

"The Mennonites drink coffee and...and ..drive? On a Sunday?" I stomped on the clutch and compromised with second gear.

"They're not Amish," Patricia told me.

"Where did they *come* from?" I asked, still bewildered.

"What do you care what they're about, dear?" Patricia said, calmer now that we were moving again.

"I don't, I guess," I adjusted my glasses. "I just...is nothing sacred?"

"Banjos and beauty queens," she conjectured, examining a nail. "Rex played the banjo you know, Johnny. He didn't think he was very good but I only ever wanted to hear *Sea of Heartbreak*. He was good at that one."

"She loved that song," I said before I could stop myself, "or I guess she was that song," I murmured angrily under my breath. I merged into a turn lane.

Patricia glanced at me. "Let's get some food in you,

dear."

I must have looked as upset as I felt. I hadn't meant to let that topic slip, but Patricia was clearly taking pity. I was uncomfortable, and mad about it. I rarely came into the city anymore. Most of my clients lived in pseudo-suburbia like me, and I didn't do commercial design. Today the city felt foreign. The hazy Sunday morning sky just made the delicate gold leaf of the Capitol dome look garish and alien. Lately anger overtook me easily and spontaneously, latching on to a triviality and burning slow until I realized what was going on and snapped out of enraged auto-pilot.

"Sorry," I told Patricia, pulling the truck into our brunch spot, "You're right, I need to eat."

That's not all I needed.

She linked an arm in mine and patted my hand consolingly as we walked to the front door of the restaurant. I looked down and was surprised by her blue eyes, which looked up at me with incorruptible concern, like a mother's would. The sudden shock of her goodness finally swept the last remnants of irritation away and I was able to put on a smile.

"Did you know Cab Calloway *hated* Dizzy Gillespie?" I asked her so she knew I felt better.

"Why you're kidding!" she said like I'd announced an existential revelation. I held open the diner door for her.

Inside, the staff was nowhere to be found. For a second we adjusted to the empty scene, Patricia blinking around and me resisting a slip back into uneasiness. The place had only opened its doors moments before and clearly didn't expect any customers so promptly. For the second time this week I felt like a trespasser.

"There was a spitball incident," I continued to Patricia as we waited for a sign of human life.

Patricia tugged my arm to seat ourselves. "They

won't *mind*," she insisted, but I resolutely held her to the foyer, maintaining at least a little order. A second later an efficient-looking hostess appeared. She was rushing and apologizing before she even reached us.

"Two this morning?" she capped off, gathering a pair of menus, and briskly led us to a bright table by a window.

"All the good people of the world are at church," I informed Patricia as we sat and the hostess left us. "Even the caffeine-drinking Mennonites. It is just you and me here, alone in our depravity." I stared at the small glass vase that sat happily between us, sporting three bouncing tulips.

"I'll show you church," Patricia told me as a teenage waitress approached. "A mimosa, please, dear," she requested before the girl could get a word in. "And listen—tell your bartender to add a little splash of Grand Marnier in that for me, would you dear? And heavy on the champagne. Thanks so much," she smiled sweetly.

"Almost heaven?" I asked from across the table.

"He wants the same," she told the girl.

"I want a coffee," I amended.

"Okay—sure," the girl scribbled nervously and half-smiled, unsure who to look at, before scurrying off.

"I'm not sure she's old enough to know what a mimosa is," Patricia frowned, removing a compact from her purse and prodding at her face in the window light.

*   *   *

Patricia was on her second drink and both of us halfway through our food when the middle-aged manager came by to personally check in with us. I figured this must be the prize you earn by being depravedly early for Sunday brunch.

"Hello folks, I'm the manager, Tom. Is everything tasting okay this morning? You enjoying the eggs benedict, sir?" He had caught Patricia in a mouthful, but I was obviously fair game.

"Oh, yes. Nice to meet you, Tom. I'm Benjamin, and this is my companion, Mrs. Robinson. The food is fantastic, thank you."

I could see him processing, and he briefly faltered as Patricia glared at me over her stack of pancakes.

"The pancakes are quite divine," she swallowed and quickly filled the silence. "What a lovely establishment you run here, Tom."

"Oh, why, thank you, Mrs. Robinson!" he beamed, successfully distracted. "Nice to meet you both. If there's anything I can do for y'all, please just let me or your waitress know." He nodded slightly and retreated to the back of the establishment out of sight. My chuckles became audible and Patricia rolled her eyes.

"You should be ashamed of yourself, Jepko," she admonished.

"He deserved it. This Hollandaise is shit," I replied.

"But the question is, did I deserve it. Here, let me try," she commanded, poking a fork at my plate.

"What—geez," I cleared my own fork out of the way just in time to avoid a collision as she helped herself to my meal.

"Where else do you need to go today," I asked, eyes wandering to a painting on the wall behind her. It depicted a makeshift bridge over a dark creek in a half-dead forest, like some sort of Kinkade from a hell dimension. It was hanging slightly crooked, illuminated on the wall by a single morning sunbeam.

"Oh, just spin me by an ATM somewhere, I have Mahjong this evening, and I need to pick up a few—Johnny?" She stopped talking as I left my seat and strode around her to the painting. I pulled a miniature level from my pocket and held it against the frame. I straightened the picture precisely, and was almost back to my seat when I turned around. Returning to the painting with a napkin, I carefully dabbed any fingerprint traces off the frame. I slowly returned and eased myself back down across from the emanating waves of Patricia's displeasure.

"You know, what I don't understand," she began, "is that I've *seen* your living room."

"That's completely different, it's a functioning file room," I explained. "*That* was a structural mistake," I pointed to the painting.

"Oh. Right. Right, of course. Hoarding isn't structural."

"Exactly."

Patricia motioned to the waitress. "Could we have our check, dear," she requested calmly.

"Right away, ma'am," the girl agreed.

"You forgot to tell me what you saw on the news this morning," I reminded her.

"Oh! Oh, you're right. Well, Dillon Meers, Johnny! They did a bit about a missing man from the Elmcroft area and so of course I turned the news up and of *course*, it was him! Apparently they have no idea how long he's been gone because he doesn't have any close family since his wife died and he worked construction—"

"How'd he afford that house?" I interrupted.

"Oh, I think it was always her money. She was a pharmacist or something. They didn't have any kids. Oh my God. You don't think it was *her* weed?! No, no, never mind, would have been too cold for it before two months ago. Plus she wasn't that kind of pharmacist. And don't interrupt Johnny, it's rude. So he worked just low-level construction and when he stopped showing up they just assumed he'd quit and I guess…" She dug around in her purse for her wallet and laid a few bills out for the waitress. "You know, really, to have everyone just assume that, he must not have had any friends."

She stopped and considered a moment. "I always knew he was a weird sort of person. Anyway his bills were all on autopay. On TV they said otherwise his credit cards haven't been used in over a *month*, Johnny, but his coworkers said he always used cash and they didn't find any cash at his house, or his driver's license or even his passport, and they have an APB out for him, and they think he ran! He *ran*, Jepko!"

She paused to throw back the last of a mimosa. "And, there's a taxi record from his house to the airport! From over a month ago! They think he ran and *nobody even knew he was gone!*" Her bright eyes were electrified with intrigue.

I wondered if anyone besides Patricia Murgatroyd would notice if I disappeared.

"Oh, and I have a date this week with Detective Giles. Actually it was Detective Giles that told me some of that. I think he knows more, too. Gonna bring it up on our date. Not that I'll be obvious about it, of course," she said.

"Of course, Patricia. I have full faith in your ability to manipulate information out of anyone alive, seasoned police officer or not. And when in the world did you have time to weasel information from the police *and* set up dates with officers of the law, anyway?"

"I called him Friday under the pretense of apologizing for my confused state on Thursday. Explained how upset I was at the passing of my beloved cocker spaniel, and that I'd had a cocktail or two to console myself."

"I didn't know you had a dog, Pat."

"Well the dog died five years ago, but I didn't discuss the timing with Detective Giles. His name was Malachi. Really was a very dear dog."

"I see. What a finely functioning alcoholic you are. Is Detective Giles aware that it's a date? And is that even legal?"

"Well of course he is, Johnny! He's taking me out to dinner. It's perfectly legitimate, I'm not a suspect in anything, after all," she looked slightly offended.

"Please forgive me, madam. Although I just don't know what I'm going to do, now. What if I need a dinner deck partner that night? Am I to grill alone? I sense my world beginning to crumble, the edges of reality loosening—"

"Do be serious, John. But you bring up a good point, I've been meaning to find you a girlfriend. If you were just a little less handsome, or less smart, or less tall...but I swear, as it is, you set a very high bar." She batted eyes at me. I suspected she wouldn't set any of her friends up with a jaded, bespectacled cynic.

"Don't bother, I would never leave you, Patricia," I said, standing and extending a hand. We headed back out to my truck, and I considered that maybe I had just needed to eat after all.

SIX

When I was nine, my father bought me my first rifle. It was a .22 intended for squirrel hunting on my uncle's property. We visited his farm on the outskirts of Kanawha County almost every weekend. Weekdays the rifle got locked up with the rest of my father's arsenal in a big wooden cabinet in the master bedroom of our townhouse. I never understood why my father didn't just keep the guns on my uncle's property. Jonathan Jepko, Senior, always implied with various posturing that I shouldn't ask, so I didn't. The row of greasy rifles stood guard over the pristine white carpet of my parent's bedroom for the duration of my childhood.

I only used the .22 once, on a deer, even though my father had told me to never use that small a caliber on that big an animal. Whenever my parents thought I was out squirrel hunting on my uncle's land I was really just out pretending I'd run away from home. I'd kick around for hidden dens and stop to dissect owl pellets. I was more interested in seeing the haphazard construction of a squirrel's nest than an actual squirrel. Sometimes I'd even start gathering sticks to construct my own shelter—free at last—before I got hungry and went home for dinner.

One of those Saturday afternoons I came upon a long-abandoned barbed wire fence along a fire road out in the forest. I guessed it was an old property marker that signified the edge of my uncle's land. The fence was still fully taut in some parts. Farther down the line, an unnatural bulge appeared in my peripheral vision.

A doe had tried to jump the wire at its highest point and gotten a hind foot snagged. She was half-dead when I got to her, hanging upside down by broken bones, unmoving except for silent, panicked eyeballs. Her emaciated form shuddered slightly as I walked towards her, making me gasp as I struggled to process what I was seeing. My nostrils filled with the smell of her blood and I almost choked. She was inextricably tangled in the barbed wire, having spent her first hours trying to escape. She'd sealed her fate in the struggle. I used my rifle that day. I never did shoot a squirrel. I just told my parents I was a bad shot.

*   *   *

On a jog the next morning I had scarcely reached the bottom of my driveway when I accidentally made eye contact with Leroy McGuff. Jogging made me feel stupid. I thought that running should be for chasing things, or being chased. But it was Monday morning, and I wasn't ready to work yet. Jogging at least eased the guilt of my procrastination.

McGuff was watering his roses with especial vigor, perhaps unaware that it was Monday. I waved to him, increasing my speed as I swung out to the road and diverted my glance. It was too late. I had only meant to study him for a couple seconds, but my gaze lingered after the wave. I heard "Hey, wait, Johnny!" boom across a rose bush at me.

I slowed to a walk and crossed the road, tennis shoes transferring from stalwart pavement to disappointing grass. Out of sight and apparently contained, a chorus of dogs took up a series of vicious howls and snarling at my approach. McGuff snatched the cigarette from his lips with a gloved hand.

"Hey," he greeted me, nodding, and then, behind him, "Clay!! Honey! SHUT IT!"

I walked to him as the dogs, to my surprise, obediently quieted. I could see the edge of a backyard fence beyond the house. A German shepherd and a golden retriever scrutinized me. I wondered if the destruction of their kennel hadn't maybe freed those dogs up a little.

Up close McGuff's belly still heaved under his overalls from the exertion of yelling. His breath smelled like smoke and cough drops. His bowl cut looked as if it belonged on one of the Three Stooges. Dark week-old facial hair extended a little too high and a little too low on his soiled face and neck. I got the distinct impression that all parts of him were hirsute and grime-coated. Beside him, a bush of delicate pink rose blooms twinkled with a excess of morning watering, mocking their nurturer.

"You seen what's been going on over at Meers'?" he asked, crossing his arms and puffing his chest out.

"Yeah. Cops talk to you?" I asked.

"Aw yeah, they came'n talked to us t'other day and the missus watched that news story on the cable." He seemed to relax now that he knew I was going to take part in the information exchange. He paused to take a drag of his cigarette before continuing. "Damndest thing I ever heard! Ain't he got nobody even noticed he was gone?" He shook his head sympathetically.

"No kidding! They think he's been gone a month or

more. I'm closest to him neighbor-wise, I guess, but I saw him so little anyway I didn't even realize it." I'd angled myself back towards Meers' house, and I mirrored McGuff's head-shakes.

"Well, he musta been in some trouble, Alma said she heard on the news they got an APB out. How the hell'd he get up to somethin' over there? You know what I think?" McGuff took another drag and leaned closer, blowing acrid smoke sideways through his teeth. "Well, Alma thinks it too: maybe they found them some new evidence, that he did kill that wife'a his. Like, somethin' they found cause they looked at things again after that note he got."

"Is that right?" I asked.

"Sure 'nough. Alma knew 'em a lil' bit and she said the missus Meers acted like she was 'fraid of him, sometimes. He was always shoutin' at her and whatnot, we could hear'em from over here at nights. Damn shame. Real damn shame if he did that," McGuff looked genuinely saddened by the thought.

"Yeah," I agreed. "I thought they'd completely cleared him, though?"

"Well you know how it is," Leroy said, lowering his voice and beginning to water again. "They said she was sad already, self-medicatin' and whatnot with drugs from her work," he paused. "But doin' that to yourself, like she did. That's an awful special kind of sad, ain't it?"

"I guess it is."

"Hey, you want some roses?" He asked suddenly.

"Uh…" I stood with my mouth open, not sure how to respond.

"Here, take some. Give 'em to your girl, the ladies love 'em." He pulled a pair of clippers from his back pocket and started severing stems. "Alma, she watches all those damn soaps and TV shows, says the sign of a nice house is fresh flowers in every room, all the gawddamn time," he sighed heavily. "Got to where it was just cheaper to grow'm myself. Sell the extras down at the flor'st though, so they pay for th'selves. Barely," he stored his cigarette in his mouth and bundled a bouquet for me. "Still gotta put time in down at the mine to afford this damn place. Here y'go, watch them thorns," he cautioned.

I carefully accepted the flowers, thanked him, and said goodbye. I walked back home slowly, wondering if McGuff would be able to see if I continued my run and chucked the bundle into the woods. I thought better of it and returned to my deck. Grabbing a mug of coffee, I headed over to Patricia Murgatroyd's backyard.

*   *   *

I caught the whiff of a few familiar but unidentifiable herbs in Patricia's garden. I trotted up the few steps to her back deck. It was a quarter of the size of mine, but screened-in. It was filled with cushioned wicker furniture and carefully arranged potted plants. I rapped on the glass window of the door to the main house. Almost immediately I heard an exclamation and sharp curse from inside.

"Who's back there!" came her muffled voice, followed by stomping footsteps.

Seconds later the door swung open and Patricia stood before me. She was holding a dripping ladle in one hand in a menacing manner. I raised my own arm and batted away a wasp.

"Oh for Chrissakes, Johnny. Not used to people coming in this way," she blustered, ushering me inside.

"I didn't want McGuff to see me," I said, immediately gaining her full attention and forgiveness.

"Didn't want who to what! Hang on, come sit in the

kitchen, dear, I was checking on the crockpot and I need a martini for this. Do you want a martini? Now explain," she commanded, eying my jogging outfit with a raised eyebrow and the hint of a smirk playing at the corner of her mouth.

I looked at my watch. It was 10:30 a.m.

"You're unbelievable," I told her. "Seriously, is Don Draper about to walk out of your bedroom?"

"I'll feed you lunch," she offered.

"Just give me the olives, you can have the gin. And yes, I'll take lunch."

"Fine."

I put down the coffee I'd brought, and grabbed a vase from an upper shelf. Filling it with sink water, I unceremoniously added the roses. I positioned the arrangement in the middle of Patricia's kitchen island and positioned myself on a barstool. I let my eyes run along the rows of souvenir cocktail glasses arrayed on racks hanging from the ceiling. The aroma wafting from the slow-cooker in the corner was already making my mouth water. I realized I hadn't eaten breakfast.

Patricia removed a jar of olives from the fridge and turned to gawk at her new island centerpiece.

"What in the hell are those, Johnny?" she asked, staring at the roses.

"Fresh flowers are a sign of an upscale household," I informed her.

"Pink roses are for Victorians," she retorted, wrinkling her nose at the flowers.

"I was told they make the ladies go crazy," I said, trying to sound forlorn.

"Uh-huh. So, spill!" Patricia commanded, sliding me over a small plate of olives. She unfolded a Sunday paper from the counter and laid it out on the island, de-layering its pages so it covered the expanse.

"Well, I think I've figured it out," I said. "I mean...sort of. Not really, I guess," I moved my elbows out of the way of her newspaper tablecloth, too afraid to ask what it was for.

"Get on with it!" She was balancing a bottle of gin over a jigger now, and I briefly paused in shock that she measured things. I tore my gaze away and continued.

"Well McGuff saw me when I left for my run and called me over, and while I was there I thought, well, I might as well see what he could see," I said.

"What?" She had inexplicably produced a bottle of spray paint. She was shaking it so violently her question was almost drowned out by the metal pea clattering about inside.

"I mean," I shouted over her clicking, "to see if he could see from his yard where the marijuana was. Well he can't. There's no way he could. That part of the yard is over a little dip from him, not to mention the trees. I could only see the driveway and front door." I paused and popped an olive in my mouth, cringing slightly. "He had about as much chance of seeing it as you or I did." I tongued the pimento.

Patricia started spraying the aerosol, as I was so futilely hoping she wouldn't. I jumped up, taking my plate of olives to the other side of the kitchen. The pink roses started to bloom metallic gold. Patricia flitted from one side of the kitchen island to the other, like she was applying last-minute powder makeup to a model. Stepping back to assess her work, she nodded curtly. She crumpled the newspaper into a ball and dunked it into a wastebasket before crossing the room to preheat the oven.

"Well that doesn't mean he couldn't have seen it some other way," she sniffed. "Knowing Leroy, he was probably Meers' dealer."

"Oh come on, Patricia," I groaned. I returned to my seat, considering the statuesque gold roses now in front of me. They glistened regally, like the capitol dome. I wondered if there was anything Patricia Murgatroyd was incapable of doing.

"Well, why not!" she exclaimed behind me, "No more shocking than our neighbor growing a *pot grove, outside*, in the middle of a *subdivision*." She drew the words out, then suddenly looked thoughtful. "I wonder if deer eat cannabis," she pondered.

"Uh-huh," I selected another olive from the plate, trying to ignore the paint fumes. "You know, I hope you didn't just throw away a Sunday crossword puzzle Anyway, two things: if that house was all his wife's money, maybe when she died he got a little desperate for extra income. And second: I've been thinking more and more the blackmail has nothing to do with his gardening habits. I mean really. You get threatened? Just pull up the damn plants and destroy them, be done with it. Abandoning your life is not even remotely necessary."

"I suppose you're right."

"And anyway, Leroy and Alma have their own theory."

"Oh, well, by all means, let's hear the McGuff theory. Yes. Yes, this ought to be good." She rapped fingernails to countertop and took a sip of her pre-noon martini.

"That he killed her," I said flatly.

"I told you already, Johnny, the girl was depressed. And the police cleared him."

"Leroy said he and Alma used to hear him shouting at her all hours of the night," I said.

"Really?" Patricia asked, looking interested.

"Yep. He said Alma knew her pretty well and half the time she seemed afraid of Dillon."

"That poor child," Patricia frowned. "I knew there

was something not right with him."

"Mmhmm. Him and Leroy both, huh?"

"Oh quit it, Johnny, that's not the same thing." She jumped a little, almost spilling her drink, as the buzzer went off to indicate the oven had reached the proper temperature.

"Well, it's something to think about," she conceded, "and certainly a more plausible reason to run. But to think. A murder in Elmcroft!" She half-shivered theatrically and crossed the room, uncovering a loaf pan of raw dough on the counter that she loaded into the oven. Closing the door, she turned back to me.

"I have my date with Detective Giles tomorrow night. Wonder if he'd tell me a little about the wife's case. I can be awfully persuasive, you know."

"Oh, I know, Patricia," I said. "Like in the way that bulls are persuasive, in china shops."

I stared at the gold roses. A tiny fruit fly landed on the wet gold paint and got stuck. I thought about that deer and about Em and I wondered if anybody around here had ever really climbed back up out of the coal mines.

SEVEN

On a Friday a year ago, I met Em for the first time. I'd taken the day off work, and planned to check the mail during what should have been my lunch hour. I didn't expect to find anything exciting in the mailbox. I didn't expect to find anything exciting outside of it, either.

I walked down the outer steps of my second story apartment and angled towards the small tower of boxes assigned to my building. The metal array was several dozen yards away across a sleepy expanse of mowed grass and empty parking spaces. Beside it was the apartment pool area. The pool itself was secured from non-residents by a locked wooden gate and a wooden perimeter fence. I unlocked the small metal door to my mailbox and emptied its contents. Then I realized there was a girl climbing over the pool fence.

She was wearing gold aviator sunglasses and office clothes. She had a white towel slung over one shoulder and an oversized purse hanging from the other. The fence was just high enough that she couldn't step over it, so she had slipped out of black heels and thrown a leg up. She pulled herself to a teetering crouch on top before hopping down on the other side. Her accoutrement banged against unconcerned hips. Long auburn hair spilled over the shoulders of her white button-up blouse. She deposited her bag on an apartment-furnished lounge chair and started shimmying out of her gray pencil skirt. It dropped, and I stared. Deft hands tied her hair in a makeshift updo out of her face.

I stood frozen, pizza coupons in hand, trying to determine whether this was a resident who had lost her key, or a bold and lovely trespasser. Beneath her discarded office clothes was a white bikini. She laid the towel out flush on the lounge chair. Then she dropped her watch in the bag and stepped waist-deep into the pool. She sunk to neck-deep and waded to one side. Backing up to the concrete barrier, she elevated her arms to the edges, closed her eyes, and leaned her head back. It looked like she was inhaling sea air instead of chlorine.

Her quick movements had seemed more efficient than nervous, as if she were on borrowed time, but wise enough to know that hurry would lead to mistakes. Streamlined. That's what I saw. That girl, I thought, didn't have a care in the world. She wasn't even there to swim. She just happened to be meditating in water. In all my life I'd never been so fascinated with a stranger. She turned suddenly and saw me through dark gold lenses. Putting one finger to her lips, she smiled and created the secret between us without uttering a word.

In the days before Em left I knew something was wrong before she even opened her mouth. But just as I had on that first day, I misinterpreted almost everything. It's man's nature to fall in love with mysteries. The allure seems holy and we can fill in the unknown with anything we want. After all, God and beautiful girls are the same.

*   *   *

"I would like to throw a sunset soiree," Patricia Murgatroyd informed me Tuesday evening.

"And how did your date go?" I repeated. It was dark, and late. My citronella candles were waning.

"It was just awful, Johnny," she finally admitted.

"Ah, yes. He wasn't a perfect gentlemen?" I asked.

"Oh well of course he was, and knew his wine, would you believe! But he didn't tell me a thing," she frowned, whirling the ice in clinking motions around her cocktail glass. Patricia had returned from her date at 8:58pm. At 9:03pm, she had appeared on my deck with nightcaps for both of us.

I slid mine back to her, feeling lifeless enough already. "Tell you what?" I prodded.

"About the case, Johnny!" She took a seat, and stared at me with wide eyes, determined to expound at her own pace. "The bastard stayed sober. I couldn't get anything out of him. That's why I need to throw a soiree."

"Right—so you can ply the officer with alcohol, and get him to reveal professional secrets." Patricia didn't look in my direction, or honor me with a response. "I'm sorry the date didn't go well," I added. I watched a moth try to kill itself on one of my defunct bug-resistant candles.

"Well I mean he was quite lovely," she said, frowning again, "He's a wonderful man. I almost thought about inviting him in...if you know what I mean." She swirled her glass again, winking at me. "Though frankly, Johnny, when you get to my age, bowel movements can sometimes be more satisfying than sex."

I tried to will my memory erased. The cat leapt onto the deck, batting at a small toad. I leaned down, scooping the struggling amphibian over the side to safety.

"So what do you think? Soiree? Johnny? ...Johnny!" Patricia stomped a foot.

"Sorry. Sorry, I was busy repressing," I said, leaning back in my chair. "What's the difference between a soiree and a cocktail party?"

"Nothing, it's just a fancier way to say it. Besides, alliteration with the sunset, you know." Pinky raised, she chugged back the last of her cocktail and added, "It's always important to sound classy."

"I see. Am I invited?" I asked, slapping a West Virginia mosquito dead on my bare foot and thinking very little about class.

"Well of course, dear, we've got to have it here," she said matter-of-factly. "You've got the outdoor speakers and the only clear view from this deck, which is, honestly, I think bigger than my living room. We'll do it Friday night, people are always so busy Saturdays, only a dozen or ten people if that, dear, you don't mind, do you? Course I don't think the sun's doing its thing till almost nine these days but we'll have them come over at eight, you know. Just a fun little cocktail hour for the neighborhood, Johnny! Oh, and could you grill up some of those little shrimp kebabs, and I'm going to make that cilantro sauce. We'll need some finger food."

Nobody ambushed like Patricia Murgatroyd.

*   *   *

Friday night I was sweating over tiny melting shrimp because, like the shrimp, I had no spine. Patricia claimed she had the guest list down to a dozen, including us. She promised me no one would enter my cluttered indoor living spaces. In return, I was going to grill fodder for her disgusting cilantro sauce. No matter that sauce for seafood should be red, not green, and also, that small talk was lethal. These are the kinds of sacrifices one makes for friends.

She got the guests who drove to park in her driveway, which was larger than mine. After a quick garden tour, she led them along a row of hastily erected bamboo torches to the side steps of my deck. It was like some sort of ceremonial grand entrance. She did not ask me to play Beyoncé over the speakers as they stepped up to the deck, so I suppose things could have been worse.

To her credit, my deck did look good. The exposed wood of the rafters and pillars took on a special hue in late daylight. My string lights caught the whitewash of the pitched ceiling far above and created a sort of effervescent glow in the cool shadows of evening. Patricia had installed various floral displays—hanging baskets in the corners, flowering vines entwining the outer rail, and single daisies in skinny bud vases on the ledges. At her bidding, there was soft jazz playing. Besides my usual outdoor dining set, we had put covers on several folding tables and pushed them up against the deck walls. The tables supported countless bottles of booze and mixers and a variety of hors d'oeuvres. Pat herself was especially colorful that night, beckoning guests with turquoise fingertips. I wondered what sort of explanation she had given them for hosting her party at my house. Then again, I didn't want to know.

Detective Giles had led the initial wave, and Patricia attached him to her arm. He looked as uncomfortable as I felt. Patricia, in fact, seemed the only one at ease, but as she herself had told me several months ago: "Oh lord, Johnny, the last time I was nervous was 1982. I think people should care what others think, but it's always been obvious to me that everyone likes me, so I don't have to worry about it at all."

Eventually Detective Giles detached himself from

her and strode to the other side of the grill next to me. With his back to the corner he folded his arms and surveyed the little crowd. I thought he looked ready to glean information concerning the missing Dillon Meers from these neighbors. The rest of the guests fanned out: some towards the hors d'oeuvres, some towards the self-service bar, and others still towards the rail and reddening sky. The sun was beginning its dive at the end of the valley, flanked on either side by Elmcroft Forest. There were already at least a dozen people on my deck. I got the distinct impression they were here for the spectacle that was Patricia Murgatroyd, not a sunset fucking soiree.

"Mr. Jepko, nice to see you again," Giles was saying. We hadn't made eye contact.

"Please, call me Johnny," I returned, taking a sort of enjoyment in his off-duty nerves.

"She force you into this too?" I asked, nodding in Patricia's direction. She was fluttering around with her usual clanging bracelets, infusing people with charisma, creating new friendships out of thin air, and setting people at ease like West Virginia's tacky female answer to Jay Gatsby. She left tinkling laughter and comfortable postures in her flame-haired wake.

"Oh God, yes," he replied, sounding relieved to have a compatriot. "That woman," he paused and shook his head. "Force of nature. Just a goddamn force of nature. Anyway, thank you for hosting, if you had a choice."

"Didn't, but it's my pleasure," I said, lying only about the pleasure. "Shrimp?"

From the corner of my eye I started my own survey of the guests. The McGuffs had not made Patricia's short list, but I recognized Jason's parents from the neighborhood. I was surprised to see Jason Controy himself, lurking against the opposite wall. He was doing a fantastic impersonation of a stunned caged animal. He caught my gaze and immediately came over, head slumped and hands in baggy pockets.

"Hi Mr. Jepko," he mumbled.

"Hi Jason, can I get you a soda or something?" I asked, wondering what had possessed Patricia to invite a teenager to an adult party with alcohol and police in attendance.

"No thanks," he said, eyes glued to the steady-glowing charcoal embers in the bottom of my grill.

"Well, nice to have you here," I said.

"Thanks. They found out I threw a party. Been grounded all week. Won't let me stay at the house by myself. They said Ms. Murgatroyd wouldn't mind," he said. Giles raised an eyebrow.

"Have you met Detective Giles, Jason?" I said, warning the teenager not to incriminate himself.

His eyes widened and he removed a hand from his pocket, offering it to Giles. "Very nice to meet you, sir," he said, suddenly alert.

"Uh huh," Giles said, accepting his hand, but Jason was already talking again.

"Well I guess I better go see how Mom is doing," he said, taking a few steps backwards before he fled to the other side of the deck.

"I'm always incredibly popular with kids," Giles said, and I honored him with a wry grin, surprised to realize I liked him.

To our right a woman I didn't know, a good-looking 50-something, had engaged Jason's parents in conversation. I assumed she was from the subdivision. The three of them had formed a tight semi-circle to one side of the deck, cocktail glasses balanced on tiny napkins in their hands. They faced out with their backs to the rest of us. David Controy, a local bank branch manager, was a short man, only an inch or so taller than his wife. He was half bald and half gray, sporting a close-cut but substantial beard that seemed at odds with his large bare forehead. He had an authoritative air about him and wore a tie. I had chosen not to wear a tie that evening.

Kim Controy looked like a caricature of the serene librarian she was. Her hair was pulled back high and neat, clothes plain but formal. Her quiet demeanor stood in stark contrast to the distinctive style of their conversation companion. If Patricia had not been present on the deck, this woman would have seemed like our idiosyncratic poster child for the evening. I later came to know her as the somewhat renowned sculptor Stephanie Michel. She was taller than either of the Controys, hovering around six feet and buoyed higher by slim knee-high boots with chunky heels. Her leggings and flowing top led to a massive head of tight curls, loosely pulled back from a face sporting hoop earrings and cat eyeglasses. As she caught my eye, I thought I saw the name Meers being mouthed. I was pulling shrimp from the grill and a resistant sizzle interfered with my casual eavesdropping, so I couldn't be sure.

"This is just lovely," said a soft but clear voice at my elbow. I turned and laid eyes on a strikingly pretty girl in her late twenties. I had every suspicion that I was beholding a special delivery. Patricia had somehow cornered a despondent-looking Jason by the shrimp dip, and did not look up to acknowledge her work. The girl looked familiar. Maybe because she appeared to have stepped out of a classic Hollywood noir, or been cloned from some mannequin in the town center mall.

"Thanks," I said, "I'm Johnny Jepko," and offered my hand.

"Oh, yes, Patricia talks about you all the time, Johnny. The book club feels like we almost know you ourselves! The lone, handsome architect," she smiled as she shook my hand with a light grip. "I'm Julia Winfield," she sang, and little diamond studs in her ears caught short bursts of the sunset and made her face sparkle. I became immediately convinced that she was going to wink at me.

"Can I get you a drink, Julia?" I asked, feeling that I needed one. I could sense Giles' eyes on my back as we walked fifteen feet to the makeshift bar.

"Vodka cranberry would be lovely, thank you," Julia Winfield told me, and tucked a strand of blond hair behind one ear, beaming. "So how long have you lived here?"

"Oh, about three months now. Not so long." I dropped ice into two glasses. "And what do you do? Besides hold the honor of keeping Patricia Murgatroyd's acquaintance, of course." I smiled, depositing the burden of conversation back on her.

"Oh, you are funny!" Julia laughed and lied, touching my left forearm and squeezing a little. I was taken aback by the contact and almost reacted, but she removed her hand as quick as she'd placed it and was already talking again.

"I'm one of the news anchors over at W-K-A-N," she was telling me. I realized she looked familiar because I'd driven past her lovely mug on one of those giant billboards right off I-79 about a million times in the last three years.

"She's quite a celebrity, Johnny. And travels sometimes for stories, does all kinds of interesting things," Patricia said as she materialized next to us.

"Very nice," I nodded at Julia, and turned to see if Patricia was done checking up on us.

"You know I can't stand boring people," Patricia said, misinterpreting my gaze.

"Except me," I pointed out.

"Yes, but you're fun to look at, dear." She harrumphed under her breath, took a sip of drink, and caught my vibe. "Well, why don't you two kids have a seat? If I don't start entertaining the detective pretty soon he might arrest me," she said, winking and sailing away.

We sat, and I started thinking what I was going to do about Julia. Em had been a just-right rough-around-the-edges. This girl was cookie-cutter beauty disguising a rehearsed personality. She'd sleep with me. It didn't matter she'd just met me, she'd decided it beforehand. I didn't know if I could stand it. I poured myself a drink to make sure I could.

"Did you grow up in Charleston?" I asked, sticking to the old dependable script.

The only person capable of missing our stationary mating dance would have been a self-involved teenager. One appeared in the form of Jason Controy, who'd been bouncing around from one uncomfortable grouping to the next. He looked relieved to find me without any police officers present. He crashed down in the seat right between Julia and I, the one I'd left open on purpose.

"They're talking about that blackmail note you found," Jason half-pointed behind him to his parents and Stephanie Michel. "I'm glad somebody found out he did it. I always knew he killed her," he sniffed, and wiped his nose with a long-sleeved forearm.

"Killed his wife?" I asked, taken aback to hear the theory from the mouth of a 17-year-old. Julia's eyes had gone wide, and she looked much less like an anchor, and much more like a reporter.

"Yeah, because of how he used to scream n' spit at her til she was just huddled up shakin' and shit. Always made me feel bad for her." He crossed his arms. "I really liked Mrs. Meers."

EIGHT

"What do you mean, Jason? Why didn't you tell anyone? Where did you see this?" As Julia commandeered the table conversation, she scooted her chair closer to the teenager's. Taking a gentler tone she said: "Jason...do you know who wrote that blackmail note?"

I wondered who else Patricia had told.

Jason visibly shrunk back, pulling his shoulders upwards. "No ma'am!" he exclaimed, sounding genuine. "He never hit her."

"Where did you see this?" Julia asked again.

"I mean I wasn't there or nothin'," Jason muttered. "I could just see the silhouettes in the windows when I was playin' ball in our driveway sometimes. Like, he'd get all close to her, wavin' his arms around, you could tell he was yellin', and sometimes she'd end up crouched up on the floor with her hands over her ears, all flinchy and shit every time he moved like she thought he was gonna hit her, him screaming like two inches from her face. But I never saw him hit her."

"Could you throw these on the grill, dear," Patricia appeared suddenly and thrust a tray of oil-slathered vegetables in front of me. She held a yogurt-y dip that smelled like lemon and garlic in her other hand, and she wasn't talking about shitty husbands.

"Sure. What...are these?" I accepted the tray, examining the contents.

"Okra, Johnny!" Patricia looked at me like I should be ashamed of myself.

"Ah...coming right up," I stood up, leaned back down close to her ear, and drawled in my best South Carolina accent: "You ever think you moved to the wrong Chawl-ston, Missus Murgatroyd?"

"Oh, of course not, Johnny," she said brightly, and then quieter, "I'm a sucker for mountain men." She cast a lascivious look toward Silas Giles, showed me her teeth, and left.

"Johnny!"

I swiveled back to the table, where Julia Winfield was glaring at me. How wonderful that she already felt comfortable enough to scold me. From my angle I got a wonderful glimpse of her cleavage. "Right...sorry, afraid I'm pre-committed to grill duties. Maybe Jason could tell Detective Giles about what he saw?"

Jason winced visibly, digging his hands deeper into his pockets.

"What a marvelous idea," Julia agreed brightly. I had fixed the situation, though I didn't know how. She corralled Jason and the two headed over to the unsuspecting detective. With a sigh I returned to the grill.

"So? Julia?" Patricia was suddenly at my side, being even more ubiquitous than usual.

"Might be more interested in the mystery of Dillon Meers than me. She's with your detective now, making the kid spill about one-sided screaming matches he used to witness from next door."

"Leroy McGuff told you they used to hear yelling too, didn't he?" Patricia paused, biting her lip.

"Yeah, I don't think it was happy-go-lucky over there." I flipped a couple okra pods.

"Patricia?" I asked after awhile.

"Yes?" she blinked out of her thoughts.

"Huh. Apparently I need to go missing to get the attention of women around here."

"Oh, honestly, Johnny. Anyway, Julia?"

"Quite lovely."

"Glad you think so. I'm afraid I brag about you a bit to the girls. Most of them are stuck hanging out with their curmudgeonly old husbands," she chortled. "Anyway, God only knows why that one's single, but I thought it might work out well for you." She smiled a smile I'm sure she thought looked innocent.

"I think you've gone and revealed yourself as a true friend," I warned her.

"Go socialize," she commanded, grabbing my tongs and hip-bumping me away from the grill.

I knew I couldn't sneak inside to solitude without Patricia catching me, so I made myself a new drink and took a spot at the rail with the other guests. They were watching the sunset, and doing their best impersonations of people that had never seen a sunset before. The name of Dillon

Meers was now on everyone's lips. He was the first mystery the subdivision had seen in five years. That's when they had discovered that the sweet, divorced single mom who lived on Mill Road was moonlighting as a stripper over at Southern X-Posure, leaving her young kids home alone on weeknights. I watched the sun disappear, and listened to all the ways Dillon Meers had apparently disappeared.

Jason Controy's parents believed Meers was dead somewhere by his own hand, heartbroken at the suicide of his pretty young wife. Perhaps he jumped off a cliff into a river, or off some high rock on the west coast. It was very tranquil there, Kim Controy suggested.

Stephanie Michel stated that Meers certainly did kill his wife. And certainly had run. And was no doubt in Mexico, although she herself would run to Croatia, of course. Then she got into a conversational tangent with Mr. Controy about bilateral extradition agreements and the stupidity of criminals. I concluded that the two of them were probably having an affair.

A professorial middle-aged man with a finely trimmed black beard, who at first glance seemed to embody intelligence, suggested Meers was vacationing in the Ozarks and had forgot to tell anybody. Or had no one to tell, and anyway would have no cell service up there. I got the impression this man's last vacation must have been in the Ozarks.

A delicate, regal-looking 70-year-old said she was sure he was killed by the Italian mafia, who, she insisted, had been present and active in West Virginia since the Hatfields and McCoys stopped feuding. "And, you know," she added after a sip of gin, "they never really *did* stop..."

Patricia's police dispatcher friend, Holly, whom we'd talked to when we'd called the cops, had arrived with her husband, Walter. They fit right in, except for Holly's hairdo, and her getting a little drunk and lighting up a Marlboro at the side of my deck. She began bragging about the pet raccoon that she'd tamed with dry dog food.

Eschewing Patricia's liquor bar Walter and Holly drank from a case of beer they'd hauled from their truck. I didn't think they quite trusted me, for which I gave them credit. Most of the guests wrote them off when Walter started talking about his factory work, but I was still listening when he switched to Dillon Meers. Meers, he said, had run because he was about to be fingered for something. It was the most reasonable assumption I'd heard.

Everyone had forgotten Jason, but now he piped up to say that Meers had probably just wandered out in the woods and gotten eaten by a bear. With that, everybody stopped talking about it.

"Gin Rummy?" Patricia polled the crowd.

"I think we're about out of snacks," I murmured to Patricia, who waved me off.

"Thanks Pat, but we've got to head back over," David Controy said, "Much appreciate the excuse to get out, as always. Johnny, this deck of yours is quite the structure," he said, shaking my hand briskly and casting about for Jason. "Time to head out, son."

"Bye, Mr. Jepko," Jason said, shuffling between his parents.

"Nice to see you all," I returned.

Beyond the deck lights night raced in, along with darkness. The guests began a chorus of goodbyes.

Julia sidled up, brushing a finger over a daisy petal. "It was very generous of you to let Patricia beflower your deck." In my head I could hear the bell announcing Round Two.

"She left me very little choice," I smiled. "Sorry I had to step away earlier."

"Quite understandable," she said, eyes soft. "So, could I have a tour of your house?"

"Only if you're very forgiving," I bargained. "You can certainly help me grab a deck of cards for Patricia, I'm sure you know how she gets when she can't gamble."

Julia and I stepped inside as Detective Giles pulled Holly and Walter to a corner of the deck. A brief interrogation began about which one of their drunk asses was driving home. Inside, Julia ignored my clutter, and indicated her intention to sleep with me. She used special phrases like "I'm sure you'll need help cleaning up" and "You must work out!"

"I jog," I revealed.

By 9:30 everyone had left except for Patricia, Julia, and Detective Giles. Patricia was unspeakably excited when the other two agreed to stay for a card game. Julia talked us into Texas Holdem, and we spent the next few hours losing to her.

"How long have you been gardening, Pat? Your vegetables look just amazing," Julia said cheerily over her growing stack of chips. I stared down at a two of clubs and seven of diamonds. Once the guests had thinned out the cat had surfaced, and now she leaned against Julia's stockinged legs, purring audibly.

"Oh! What a sweet little thing," Julia smiled down

and gave the cat a rub.

"Want her?" I offered.

"Ignore him," Patricia said without looking up from her cards. "To answer your question, Jules, I've been gardening for five years and I plan to quit in another five."

I watched Silas Giles slowly look up from his hand, and even more slowly turn to look at Patricia, who did not return his gaze.

"I do whims by the decade," she explained without looking up.

"You're lucky you met her now," I said, honoring him with eye contact, "Last decade it was moonshine."

"It was nothing of the sort," Patricia said as Julia giggled.

"My mistake," I apologized to the table at large.

It certainly wasn't a mistake. She'd informed me of her moonshine habit a month ago while wasted on tequila. "Can you believe?" she'd reminisced on my deck, "The agents even put out this official report calling it a 'clear, pale yellow-green liquid' with a 'new and raw bouquet.' Like they were goddamn sommeliers, of all things!" Patricia had snorted. "I just called it my Christmas Cheer."

*   *   *

I was standing in my kitchen staring at a glass of water when I heard the early morning commercial jet to Atlanta rumble overhead. Somewhere down the street a braking garbage truck shrieked. My heart beat fast like I was guilty of something, but I told myself I was just suffering from too much alcohol and too little direction. I returned to my room and crawled into bed next to a fast-asleep Julia Winfield. She was barely draped in sheets and looked like a beautiful, terrible, naked angel. The calico cat was curled benignly at her feet, as if they both were home. I fell asleep feeling nauseous to the sounds of the world waking up.

For a couple hours I dreamt fitfully about the first time I spoke to Em. It was the Monday after I first saw her. I had taken my lunch break at home, and made sure to check my mail at the exact same time that I had the past Friday. Defying my cynical expectations, she was already laid out on a lounge chair by the pool when I walked over. I walked right up to the fence and leaned my elbows over the top.

"Do you want my spare key?" I asked, seeing the distant placement of her tossed shoes.

She pushed herself up and looked at me. "I don't think I know you nearly well enough," she said evenly, betrayed only by the slightest twitch at the corner of her mouth. I smiled and knew I loved her.

"I'm Johnny," I said.

"Nice to meet you, Johnny."

"And you must be...Em?" I said when she stayed silent.

"Em?"

"M, for Mermaid," I smiled. She laughed.

"Yes," she said, "I think I like that."

To my surprise she rose and walked over, extending a hand up to the fence. I shook it, realizing we were both left-handed. And that she was wearing a wedding band. M for Mermaid. M for Married.

It's a recurring nightmare.

NINE

"I hope you don't mind me using your pool," Em said, turning, and leaning her back against the fence. She looked out over the marbled turquoise. "I work at the pharmacy up the road, and I'm not big on break rooms."

"Not in the least," I assured her. "I really do have a spare pool key you can have. I rent a double, so they gave me two, but it's just me."

"Is this your lunch break, too?" she asked, regarding me suddenly.

"Yeah. I like to come home for lunch. I work over at Lomax & Associates."

"The architects?"

"Yep."

"Tell you what," Em said. "Instead of giving me your spare, why don't you bring your key and meet me for a swim tomorrow. I'll bring a picnic." She glanced at me sideways and grinned.

I adjusted my glasses and tried to hide my surprise. "Well, okay," I replied.

"Noon?"

"Noon it is," I agreed.

"See ya Johnny," she said abruptly. She straightened up from the fence and stepped quickly back to her chair. I watched her gather her things before turning back to my apartment to consider the invitation. She had sounded calm, rather than flippant. She had seemed certain. I didn't know I was witnessing the kind of enlightenment that comes with hitting rock bottom. Then again, what other kind of enlightenment is there?

Anyway, a couple months after that I taught her how to use a gun. I knew she'd never use it on me.

*   *   *

I had just come back from a job site in Elkview on Monday and was about to pull onto my property. Then I looked down Dillon Meers' driveway. Realizing there was someone in it, I turned down there instead. I'd been feeling a little reckless ever since Julia Winfield had scurried off half-embarrassed half-satiated early Saturday morning while I pretended to still be asleep. I didn't relish her apparent assumption that ours might be a budding relationship. If she pressed me, I would be forced to explain that I was pre-ruined, incapable of love, and she shouldn't waste her time. But she hadn't said anything, or even called.

I eased my pickup forward, squinting to determine the identity of the figure at Meers' front door. It was a male, but he didn't look like a cop. He was close to my age, and similarly built. He was ducking to look into windows and shuffling back and forth at the door, laying the occasional tenuous finger on the crime scene tape as if to test its elasticity. He had just pulled something out of his pocket, and deftly replaced it when he heard my engine. It had looked like a small brown case. My money was on a lock pick set, or maybe he was just getting out a wallet to leave his card. Maybe. He turned in a casual manner and lifted a hand to wave, walking towards my truck.

"You seem lost," I said, leaving the truck running, as I stepped out onto the driveway.

"Well, hey there." He smiled broadly like he hadn't heard, and sauntered a few steps toward me. His jeans were on the baggy side. Well-tanned arms shrugged from an old white Metallica t-shirt. His eyes seemed more threatening than his smile.

"I'm looking for Dillon," he said, offering me a hand, "I'm Zebulon Fix. Zeb for short." He smiled brightly at me as we shook hands. I thought he could probably kill me if he wanted to, but I appreciated the act.

"Johnny Jepko. Neighbor. I don't think he's in there," I offered, glancing over his shoulder to the front door.

Zebulon Fix laughed. "Ha! Well, no, I reckon not." He stuffed his hands into his pockets. "What all's been happenin' around here?" He nodded back toward the house.

"He's missing. Police intercepted some sort of blackmail note. They're looking for him, too." I watched for a reaction, but he didn't give me one.

"That so," Zeb said, and pulled a can of Skoal out of a back pocket, packing it against his palm. His baggy jeans were more for utility than fashion. This guy knew perfectly well Dillon Meers was missing.

"Can I ask why you're looking for him?"

"Oh, well, me and Meers, we go way back. Haven't seen him in awhile. Seems his phone got cut off. I was in the neighborhood and thought I'd swing by, see what was up," Zeb explained. I realized his car must be the shitty Honda I passed out on the main road. He'd had the foresight to park far away from a crime scene he supposedly knew nothing about.

"Huh," I responded. "Well listen, there's a detective on the case who comes around now and then. Want me to pass along your info so he can keep you updated?"

"Oh lordie, no, boss, 'fraid I'm a little too fond of the grass. The cops and me are forever gettin' into misunderstandings. Tell you what, *you* could do me a big favor, though." His smile never faltered.

"Sure," I said, after a brief pause.

"Lemme give you my number—you look like a perfectly respectable citizen, know what I mean? If you hear anything and let me know, I'll see if I can't return the favor sometime."

"Alright, I can do that," I said. We exchanged numbers. I wondered what Zebulon Fix could possibly think he could ever do for me.

"And now if you'll excuse me, I have an altogether impatient canine waitin' in the car, best be on my way." He turned to go and I saw the handle of what looked like a 9mm tucked into the back of his ever-surprising pants.

"Oh, Zebulon?" I called after him, and he stopped.

"Call me Zeb," he said, turning.

"They confiscated the pot plants, Zeb." I told him.

The corner of his mouth pinched up briefly in a smirk and his eyes flashed, and then he smiled broadly at me again.

"I knew you was a respectable sort of citizen, didn't I." He turned the corner onto the main road and disappeared.

I walked back to my truck and looked up to see Leroy McGuff staring across the street at me.

I shrugged at him. "I don't know," I said loudly.

Leroy McGuff didn't say a goddamn word.

*　　　*　　　*

It wasn't too long before people started assuming Dillon Meers was dead. Or at least Patricia did. I spoke to Detective Giles and related my encounter with Zebulon Fix. "You did good, son. We're...acquainted...with Mr. Fix," Giles had told me, and I could almost hear his index finger stroking his mustache thoughtfully on the other end of the line. "Keep your distance if he comes around again, and let me know."

"Never used a single credit card," Patricia explained. "Plus that airplane ride was bogus!" She laughed and poured me a little more daiquiri. Her strawberries were ripe this week.

"What do you mean, the airplane ride was bogus?" I asked, sipping the drink she gave me and leaning back into the shade of my deck.

"I mean he got a taxi or Uber or whatever it is from here to the airport, had a plane ticket," she paused, licking drops from her thumb. I cringed.

"And?" I prodded.

"Right, dear, well he never got on the plane, can you believe?" She laughed, "They've traced him *going* to the airport. But from what Silas told me the other day, he never left it. He never flew!"

"So he never left," I said.

"He never left," Patricia repeated, eyes aglow. Then she glanced to her right and left, like Dillon Meers could be anywhere. In fact, he could.

"Columbo would already know who did it," she commented.

"Who? Did what?" I asked, regretting it immediately.

"Know who killed Dillon Meers," Patricia said

authoritatively.

"How do we know he's dead?" I asked Patricia.

"Oh honey, he didn't fly away. So where else would he be but dead?" Patricia made it sound very logical.

"Um...disguising his escape as a flight, but really taking off elsewhere? Pretending to run so no one would look for him locally? Going completely underground?" I made these sound more logical.

"You've not seen the news, have you dear," Patricia sympathized.

"You know I don't own a TV. Why would I have—"

"Come on, Johnny," she'd grabbed my hand and was already leading me across the grass to her garden and through it on up to her back porch. I followed her through the back door into her living room. After seating me on her plush white couch she started making drinks in the kitchen. Wondering what the couch was covered with, I punched at it a little. With a remote from the kitchen, Patricia switched on her TV. The local news sprang to life in front of my face.

"The search continues for missing Elmcroft resident Dillon Cyrus Meers, last seen at his residence sometime in April," said the immaculately attractive blonde that had slept in my bed last Friday night.

"You timed this," I accused Patricia immediately.

"You haven't called her," Patricia said, denying nothing.

"She hasn't called me," I punched the couch again, recognizing a no-win situation.

"I thought you said she was lovely."

"I thought you knew I was broken."

Patricia came around from the kitchen and sat on the other side of the couch. She handed me the drink in her left hand and took a sip from the one in her right.

"Why do they think Meers is dead," I asked,

suddenly tired.

"Oh, they don't really. I do. Johnny, dear. I won't make you stay. I don't think you're broken, but I won't press you on why you feel that way. We are friends, you and I. And I don't need to know everything. And I'm sorry I interfered in your love life, but sometimes I wonder, how content can you be only hanging out with an old coot like me? I was just trying to find you some companionship, dear. I know you stay polite and pretend to like me but surely—"

"You are all I need," I said, more emphatically than I meant to. "If I didn't like hanging around you I would...make you go away."

"Well isn't that comforting," Patricia said, raising an eyebrow.

"Sorry."

"You know, you shouldn't have slept with her, then," she said, still bold enough to sound reproachful.

"Well, it's the damnedest thing," I said.

"What?"

"She's so fucking hot," I said, pointing at the TV.

Patricia Murgatroyd asked me to leave her house. She told me I could take the glass with me, and that I shouldn't come back until she'd remembered enough good things about me that I seemed classy to her again.

I went out and sat in her garden right between the aging strawberries and the sensitive rosemary. I finished my drink while I poked at bugs. I realized she'd been giving me the break. After fifteen minutes she felt sorry for me, and cracked the porch door. She yelled for me to come back inside. She was making dinner.

She threw a towel down on the white couch so my dirty khakis wouldn't soil it. Feeling like a domesticated pet, I picked up a book from her coffee table. The cover informed me God had ascribed certain gifts and flaws to each particular astrological sign. I was drunk on vodka, so I opened it. I turned to Aquarius and was told I'd been given the gift of freedom, but "You will have the pain of loneliness, for I do not allow you to personalize My Love."

"I wouldn't even love God," I shouted to Patricia in the kitchen.

"That's not what that means," she shouted back, stirring something in a big pot. As usual, she wasn't looking. I couldn't really see her, anyway, because the sparkling gold roses were in the way.

TEN

Em was the kind of girl who had never known pain, so she tried to create her own. She was born into the tragedy of two loving parents who never divorced. She was smart, but allowed herself to be constantly underappreciated, because she didn't feel she had time for self-promotion. She had married the first guy who asked her. She'd done well in school, was starting a great career as a pharmacist, and only abused the merchandise when things at home were really, really unbearable. It would have been better to leave her husband, but the possibility never occurred to her. She let the world break her. She thought it appropriate. She had a lot of views about what was appropriate. I could tell the chemicals floating around in her beautiful head had been against her from the start, but I didn't say anything. She was too long and too far into it.

We hung out at the pool every lunch break for weeks. Those half hours were the favorite times of my life. I would pull up my sleeves and loosen my tie and gaze at her from a lounge chair while she intermittently swam, floated, and talked about the colors she saw when she closed her eyes. She was as interested in the nature of evil as the life cycle of Madagascar moths. I'd have been a fool to mistake her passion for whimsy. My own strange, private mermaid. She didn't think me appropriate, but I was her one shining exception. One day she said she was being forced to take some vacation time, and did I want to as well, and we could spend all day at the pool. I did, but we spent no time at the pool. She arrived before dawn and I met her in the dark at the shadowy pool fence and I asked her back to my apartment for coffee. We never had coffee, either. But when I kissed her, the sun came up.

*   *   *

Patricia was the first one to notice that the clutter in my living room was seeping out into other portions of the house, and she lost no time in pointing it out.

"Johnny. Your...collection is growing. Did something happen to you, John?" she asked, suddenly serious, peering around a corner of stacked paperwork in the living room. When she hadn't found me outside on the deck she'd invited herself in through the unlocked glass door.

In the kitchen I looked up from the sandwich I was preparing.

"Hi," I said. "Would you like a sandwich? Liverwurst and lettuce."

For a woman that could handle her liquor, she looked vaguely nauseated. "Dear God, Jepko. I really don't know why I let you feed yourself."

"What do you mean 'has something happened to me'? I was feeding myself long before you came along, Patricia," I defiantly ground pepper over the open sandwich while meeting her gaze.

"It's July 1st," she said, ignoring me. "Did you say 'rabbit rabbit rabbit' when you woke up?"

"Oh, shoot, no. Was out on the deck with my morning coffee and thought to, but I was too distracted by the sight of all the rabbits helping themselves to your garden in the morning sunlight. At that point it seemed really redundant to invoke any more."

I ducked by her before she could swat at me. Vaguely fuming, she followed me through the stacks back out to the deck.

"Your...clutter...is spreading," she reiterated, calming herself as she reached down to unstick a newspaper page from the heel of her stiletto. I fervently hoped it wasn't a Sunday crossword puzzle. I knew I should really start filing those.

"I work from home," I told her. "It's all stuff I need."

She eyed me sadly, and that rankled me more than anything.

"Why don't you go enjoy your *own* lunch on your *own* deck, Patricia," I snapped.

Her mouth tightened but she didn't look angry. She didn't say anything, either.

"Have a good afternoon, Johnny," she finally said, unusually formal, and left. I wallowed in guilt and dread as I watched her step down from my deck and walk to her house. I hadn't asked what she'd wanted in the first place. I unceremoniously heaved my sandwich over the rail, listening to it swish and gently plunk down at the edge of my property, and I wondered if the squirrels or raccoons would get to it first. I didn't care. I wasn't hungry anymore.

*   *   *

Three hours later I had gotten a little work done, calmed down, and wholly regretted my actions. I drove to the nearest convenience store and pulled a cheap bottle of Pinot Grigio from the shelf, and then put it back, and grabbed a cheap bottle of Merlot instead. I shoved cash at the skinny woman behind the counter who smiled at me with a mouth only half full of teeth. I drove home and walked over to Patricia's with the bottle and two wine glasses I'd procured from the far back of one of my kitchen cabinets.

I had gotten in the habit of using her back porch door, and she didn't seem to mind too much anymore. I freed a couple knuckles from the glasses to rap a couple times. I could hear intermittent shuffling inside but it was almost a full minute before the door opened. Patricia stood, staring at me. She held a highball glass at a precarious angle in one hand, and replaced her other hand on a jutted hip after opening the door. Dried mascara was frozen in blotchy trails under dry eyes, like she'd been crying, but not in the last hour. Her bright red hair was spiked at odd angles and she was only wearing one earring. Her heels had been replaced with rubber garden clogs.

"Christ, Patricia," I blurted out.

"What do you want, Johnny," she slurred tiredly.

"Peace offering," I half-stated, half-asked, raising the bottle and glasses.

She eyed the wine bottle and opened the door further, stepping back so I could enter. I edged around her carefully.

"Look, Patricia, I'm really sorry. I didn't mean to be rude. Well, I did mean to be rude. I just get—well look, I'm really sorry I upset you so much, and—"

"Oh for fuck's sake Jepko, you didn't upset me," she said, and the corner of her mouth twitched.

"I...didn't?" I said, eying her skeptically.

"Well, you did act like an utter neanderthal, but honey, you're only male." She patted me on the back and took a lengthy sip from her glass.

"How considerate of you to handicap us," I said, entering her kitchen and fishing about her drawers for something to open the wine. I turned around to find she'd already pulled a hinged waiter's corkscrew from her pocket. She commandeered the bottle, and wrenched the cork out with a small pop.

"Look honey," she said, all blustering efficiency as she poured the wine. Slightly over-extended pronunciation belied her higher-than-usual state of inebriation. "We all have our issues. The human brain is a very difficult thing to please, if you ask me." She paused and tasted the wine. "Jesus Johnny, did you buy this at a gas station?"

"...Yes," I admitted after a moment.

"No matter. Anyway, your issues are none of my business unless you want them to be, and that's fair enough. And today is a very special day for me, it's Rex and my anniversary, see, and that has nothing to do with you so you don't need to worry about it. It just happens to mean I'm having a bad day is all. Thank you for the wine."

"You're welcome," I said, thinking the last thing she needed was more alcohol. I looked beyond her at a framed photo on the living room wall of her and Rex on their wedding day. It was a grainy black-and-white shot from the seventies when Patricia was in her early twenties. She'd aged well, but all the various hints and subtleties of aging beauty in her face today were featured at large in the photo. Her blue eyes were translucent like glass in the grayscale, smile bright, cheekbones skyward, expression pure joy. She looked like the ideal of something. The slightly older handsome man holding her arm was clean-shaven and dark-haired. His eyes spoke of intelligence and his smile hinted of satisfaction and thirst at the same time. I supposed Patricia had loved Rex Murgatroyd quite a lot. I supposed she might miss him even more.

"Tell me about him," I said, selecting one of the wine glasses and taking her elbow to escort her to the couch.

"Oh, I don't know Johnny," she said, sounding sad.

"I'll tell you about the girl," I said, cursing in my head.

Her eyes brightened. "You will?"

I sighed. "Yeah. Go wash your face, you look scary."

"I can already assume she had a high tolerance for tactlessness," Patricia called back on her way to the bathroom, developing a lisp at the last word.

I sat on the couch and fiddled with the remote control, realized it was late afternoon, and half-heartedly left the television on a local channel playing national reruns. The wine was terrible. I realized I'd still not had lunch and wandered back into the kitchen to see if there was anything in the crock pot. There wasn't. I opened the fridge, which was well stocked with nothing of substance.

"You didn't eat that horrible sandwich, did you?" Patricia said from behind me. Her hair looked a little more managed now, the lone earring removed, and all traces of eye makeup wiped clean.

"Got distracted," I lied.

"I don't cook on Wednesdays," she matter-of-factly announced. "Pizza?"

"Sure," I agreed.

"Maybe your cheap Merlot will complement cheap pepperonis, eh?" She picked up a phone and overzealously clinked her liquor glass with my wine.

"Right," I blinked and steadied my drink.

"What vineyard are these from, Johnny?" She asked, suddenly grabbing the glass from my hand, and stared at the logo while her shoulder propped the phone to her ear.

"Pretty cool little place, actually, it's a winery with an attached greenhouse off of the tasting room. Has an elevated plank floor with cafe tables and chairs set up all around all the exotic plants, so you can sample your wine and pretend you're in the Amazon. Great view too, on top of a hill looking over a—"

"Yes! Yes, hello dear, it's Patricia Murgatroyd. I'd like to order a large pepperoni for delivery. And some of those garlicky sticks, you know. And you all still haven't gotten salads, have you? That's really a shame, you know, I'm sure they'd be very popular. Doesn't make any sense that you have Ranch dressing and no salads. Yes, I'll hold." She leaned the phone back on her shoulder and looked impatiently at me. "Well? A hill overlooking what?"

"Oh—a lake. Just a lake," I continued. "It was one of Em's favorite places to go, when we found time."

"Em, huh," she smiled at me. I could hear the crackle of a voice on the other end of the phone. Patricia began reciting her address and phone number in excruciatingly drawn-out syllables, until she was stopped by another crackle.

"What do you mean you already know my address!" she snapped into the phone. "Oh. Oh, I see. Well I don't know if I like being 'in the system,' young man." She brought her drink up and paused to take a sip. "I see. Very well then. That's all. I'll pay with cash." She replaced the phone on its receiver. "Do you have any cash on you, Johnny?" She said, looking up at me again.

*   *   *

If the bready meal had any influence on Patricia's sobriety it was hard to tell. We both ate our fill and returned to the couch, trading stories of Rex and Em well into the night. Patricia didn't stop drinking the hard stuff. She interrupted herself occasionally with a gasping choke of tears, knees pulled up tight to her chin and arms wrapped in a self-embrace. She curled her socked toes into the couch cushion like she was tunneling to some sort of salvation.

"Rex always wore a tie too, you know," she smiled, reaching over to run a few fingers down my own. "It's how I knew you were one of the good ones the first time I met you, Jepko." I wondered what would catch up to her first, weariness or the alcohol.

Once the levee broke I found it easier and easier to talk about Em. Patricia was actually a good listener—sometimes—and for once she didn't pester me with questions I didn't want to answer. It grew dark outside and the television still droned quietly across the room as our conversation lulled. Leaning slightly back on the couch, Patricia closed her eyes and surrendered herself to dreams. I hoped for her sake they were of Rex, and not the loss of him.

The TV suddenly took on more volume as a special news alert bulletined across the screen. I looked up to see Julia Winfield in all her perfection orating seriously to the camera: "Again, an arrest warrant has been issued for one Dillon Meers, lately of Elmcroft Subdivision, who the police are now reporting is a suspect in the death of his wife, Darby Meers. Up until recently, Darby Meers' death this past December had been ruled a suicide, but police have reopened the case based on as yet undisclosed evidence. There is an APB out for Mr. Meers, who has not been seen in months and is suspected of fleeing the area. Any information the public can provide as to his whereabouts is greatly encouraged. If sighted, please under no circumstance approach Mr. Meers, who is considered dangerous. Call 9-1-1 or your local police departme—"

I fumbled for the remote and punched hard at the power button, cringing at the static hiss the television made powering off. Hearing it, Patricia stirred beside me, then sat up, sleepy eyes on me.

"Oh, so sorry dear, must have drifted off." she said, "Why, what happened to the TV, Johnny? You must be so bored here in the quiet! You go on home dear, you don't have to worry about me."

I sighed heavily.

"Okay, Patricia. You have a good night."

I collected my wine glasses and exited through the back. I tried to rid my mind of guilt, but like a wet towel after wringing, it stayed saturated.

M for Mermaid. M for Married. M for Meers.

I stumbled home in the dark.

ELEVEN

I thought about going to bed, because I was drunk and tired and scared. But the fear took over and I thought about all the things I had done wrong. I couldn't stop. I thought about that day Em had dragged me to the gun range, and how uncannily interesting her smile was. It was wise and sweet and lit up in all kinds of unexpected ways. The last time I remember it was from that particular afternoon.

I knew she was married, but like many things, we didn't talk about it. We'd had a brief laugh about the fact that neither of us had Facebook pages, and then we extrapolated that into never even exchanging phone numbers. We were far more personal than numbers.

We met on an early December morning, sepia chilled and windblown. She brought the gun I knew was probably her husband's. She confirmed it with a quip about its owner too frequently being at the intersection of stupid and mean—the kind that don't realize women can be trusted with such instruments.

"I don't want it getting into the wrong hands," she

said, but I didn't understand what she meant.

I cupped my cotton-encased hands over her bare ones and taught her how to aim, and stand, and shoot. We co-fired the little pistol with remarkable precision until she coughed. It was a bad kind of cough. I drew back to see what was the matter.

"I'm sorry...nose bleed," she said, handing the gun to me and turning away in an embarrassed, desperate manner. She'd never seemed desperate before. I turned her head back around and held a gloved hand under her nose, catching the trickle of blood. I put my other arm around her. That was when she smiled, through the blood.

"Do you get these often?" I asked, because I saw her almost every day but that wasn't often enough.

"Just the weather," Em said, hanging onto my arm like I was her only means of support.

"Let's go," I said, and we headed back to my truck. I retrieved a plastic bag from the passenger floor and peeled my gloves off into it. I got her situated with her head back and eyes to sky, looking peaceful.

"I love you, Johnny," she said, like her head wasn't bleeding.

*   *   *

"We're going to be late," I said into my cell phone, easing into a coil-spring chair.

"They don't set off the fireworks till it gets dark Johnny, honestly." Patricia echoed loudly on the other end, sounding as if she had the speakerphone turned on in a bathroom.

"It'd be nice to find seats before it gets dark," I grumbled back, and then my phone beeped to indicate I'd been hung up on. I put the phone down and put my head back and studied an abandoned spider web between two of the deck rafters. Dust and grimy bug particulates rendered it starkly against the whitewash. It was the opposite of the early morning dewy kind. I heard Patricia's back door slam and she stepped up onto the deck a moment later.

"Well let's go," she said, heaving the strap of a blue cooler bag tighter around her shoulder. "Have you got the chairs in the back of your truck?"

"Yes ma'am," I answered, staring at her outfit. She had a red and white striped blouse fitted loosely over a long blue skirt featuring a white star pattern. A blue scarf was tied lightly around her neck, and thick red-rimmed sunglasses mirrored red heels, red nails, red earrings, red hair. It looked like patriotism had thrown up on her.

"You look nice," I said, "and...appropriate."

"Thank you, dear. And I guess this is you being appropriate?" She gestured at my clothes.

I looked down at my light blue button-down and khakis. "It's blue," I noted of my shirt.

"Mmmhmm. Well let's go before the ice melts, Julia's meeting us there with the girls," Patricia said. She started across the deck towards my truck.

"What?" I grabbed my keys off the table and followed her, punching the unlock button with slightly more force than was necessary.

"It's Saturday night, Johnny, I do have certain social obligations. Besides, Jules lives right down the road from the Pavilion; she was already going." She paused to put the cooler in the back bed of the pickup. "I just told her you asked if she could sit with us," she added, quickly hopping in the cab and closing the passenger door.

I stood outside the driver's side, gritting my teeth. I finally got in and stepped on the clutch, starting the truck and saying nothing. I pulled slowly out of the driveway.

Patricia helped herself to the radio dials and used her fingers and inestimable powers of influence to immediately locate a crackling rendition of *Walking on Sunshine*.

"Isn't this fun!" She exclaimed, slapping me on the arm.

Nobody ambushed like Patricia Murgatroyd.

*   *   *

Drexler Pavilion was locally considered an event venue, but I considered it a very large and mostly unkempt field. The University of Charleston had bought it up to spare it from trailer parks and cattle farming. It was always muddy and shit-covered anyway. There was a structure, of sorts, that passed itself off as the "pavilion" part. It couldn't be called ramshackle, but it was certainly rudimentary. It was really just a very large concrete slab topped with cheap columns and a cheaper roof. It had about as much in common with the Parthenon as dandelions had with orchids. I had never seen anyone from the University of Charleston anywhere near it.

It was about half an hour outside the city, but only ten minutes down the road from us. For many years it had been the location for a fireworks show, ideal for those that didn't like to socialize in the city on Independence Day. Half the field was dedicated to parking. By the time we arrived, I pulled the Tacoma in to join forty or fifty other vehicles already secured on grass off the main dirt road. We parked and unloaded. Patricia swung the cooler back to her shoulder, and I grabbed a folding chair under each arm. I followed her into the fray of people.

The sun was beginning to set. Patricia resolutely navigated through a sea of camo, cigarette smoke, careening children and baseball hats. We reached the one small gathering of locals who weren't holding beer bottles. This group was decked out in ultra-patriotic attire, although—depending on how you defined patriotic fashions—none quite as patriotic as Patricia.

"Yoohoo! Amy dear! Oh hi! Sherry! Julia!" As Patricia started gushing greetings I held back, dropping the chairs down so they leaned against my legs while supported by solid ground. The pavilion was off to our left, unused except for its elevated speakers. They were playing country music at a high volume, but not high enough to compete with the throngs of people around us. Off in the distance at the very end of the field, maybe fifty yards away, I could see a small group of men setting up an intimidating row of explosives. I tried to gauge which way the wind was blowing with a surreptitiously wetted finger, but to no avail. I hoped that meant there wasn't any wind.

I knew lurking on the sidelines was a recipe for an even worse disaster. Just as Patricia was finishing off her flurry of hellos I picked up the chairs and stepped forward. It was a semicircle of about half a dozen women. I started unfolding the chairs and eying the cooler.

"This is Johnny Jepko, ladies, for those that don't know," Patricia announced, pausing to wink at Julia while she backed up a step and put an arm on my back. "My delicious neighbor. Isn't he just too much! Very talented architect, you know."

"Oh, THIS is the neighbor!" several voices said in unison. I was presented with several hands which I shook in turn, half-heartedly trying to remember names. And then suddenly the hands were gone, and all eyes were back on Patricia. Only Julia, glowing near my side in a white sundress, half glanced at me in a sorry sort of way. Well, I thought, this wasn't so bad.

"So anyway, Pat," the woman called Amy was saying, "I had to fire the poor thing. I mean she forgot to plug in the machine, for Christ's sake. The battery died, and so did the patient."

"What hospital do you work for, Amy?" Julia immediately ducked in, and my potential ally vanished to the cluster.

With centripetal force Patricia commandeered the circle, all members looking to her. They kept a reverential distance, talking amongst themselves, but pulled back intermittently to check in and garner a comment from her. I almost wondered how they'd functioned before she arrived. I sidled up and gave her a look.

"One sec dear," she said, reaching down to her cooler and yanking one of the folding chairs closer for a seat. She used the other folding chair as a bar surface to make my drink. I didn't know where I was going to sit, but I didn't complain when she handed me a whiskey and coke in a clear plastic cup.

Once the drink was safely in my hands I asked quietly, "You had me crash a girl's night, to see Julia again?"

"Oh no, dear! I needed a ride," Patricia smiled sweetly. "Besides, Johnny, really. You know I'd rather spend my fourth of July with you around. It's rather lonely at the top."

"I'm going to wander before the fireworks start," I replied.

I circumvented clusters of people like a cat picking its way around puddles. I eventually made my antisocial way to the outskirts of the field, where I turned my back to the crowds and watched a few sun rays making their last stand.

"Johnny Jepko?" I heard behind me. I turned. Zebulon Fix was grinning at me, Bud Light bottle in hand.

"Well hi," I said, "we meet again."

"I usually try'n avoid fireworks," he stepped up to me, "but I make an exception for this particular variety," he winked.

"Ah. Have you been out here for this show before?" I asked. I adjusted my glasses as he hawked a stream of dip spit onto some unsuspecting grass blades.

"Oh, yeah. I come to 'bout everything here. I live right down the road, first trailer park on the left. You know, the one with all the elaborately carved verandas and terraced gardens out front," he gestured illustratively with his hands, painting designs in the air.

When I blinked he slapped me on the back.

"I kid, boss," he said. "It's a shit pile."

We chatted for a few minutes. I decided I liked Zebulon Fix, but with that kind of detached admiration I usually reserved for tigers in shoddily built cages. He stepped back to his friends and I headed back to the gaggle of women as darkness began to set in. They were easy to find. The pitch of their voices was drowning out the whoops of the crowd in a feat only martini-fueled housewives can accomplish. I tried to will away the foreboding sense of emasculation.

Julia sidled up as I returned, still glowing, and notably not noisy. She touched her plastic cup to mine. She smelled like something I wanted to lick.

"I heard you were desperate to sit beside me at this little shindig," she said, looking ahead and not at me. "You afraid of fireworks, Jepko?"

"Oh, no. Thought you might be." I said.

"You've been misinformed. But then, I suspect we both were," she contributed.

"I think you may be right." I took a sip of rum.

"So can I have a ride back to your place tonight? I plan on getting terribly drunk," she said calmly.

Well, since she put it that way.

"If you don't mind squeezing in the cab between Pat and me," I risked a look at her. "The quarters will be...close."

She smiled at me and moved away, resuming her usual practice of asking people questions like she was researching a role.

A woman approached me, and I was surprised to see she looked to be somewhere around Patricia's age. I hadn't been aware Patricia hung out with her peers.

"Hi Johnny, I'm Sherry. Patricia's friend. You know, the one she never mentions." Sherry smiled genuinely from under long, dark, gray-streaked hair. She was taller than Patricia, and had a thick accent, but her entire demeanor seemed a still lake to Pat's roiling oceans.

"It's very nice to meet you, Sherry. She only mentions me because I drive her places," I offered.

"Oh, no, honey. She mentions you because you're very nice to look at."

"I keep hearing that," I said.

"Anyway, I'm glad you've provided her with some drinking company. Don't touch the stuff myself, and hate for her to do that alone. Just not very healthy for body or mind. But I don't mean to lecture. I can tell you're a good man, Johnny. Good influence." She patted my arm in a motherly way. She sighed through a smile and turned away, floating her delicate mannerisms elsewhere.

"They're starting, Johnny," Patricia pulled me to my seat as the first burst of crackles boomed into the night sky. "Here we go!"

Julia pulled up a chair on my other side.

"In case you develop some sort of latent fear," she explained.

"Aren't you considerate," I said, staring at her cleavage again.

Julia Winfield leaned to whisper in my ear. "You don't know the half of it."

Sherry raised a glance to us across the semicircle. At

first she was only visible by her silhouette, but I saw a burst of red fireworks reflected off her face. She looked concerned. I didn't know which one of us she was concerned for.

TWELVE

"Because it's such a *cliché* for a single person to have a cat," Julia explained when we got home after the fireworks show. We had dropped Patricia off at her own house and retired to mine for a supposed nightcap.

"I thought you were joking about the terribly drunk part," I eyed her.

"I'm not that drunk, Mr. Jepko," she said as she kicked off her heels in my kitchen. I considered her a moment. "Will you keep the heels on?"

"Will you name her 'Cliché'?"

"Yes ma'am."

Julia stepped back into her heels and reached around to unzip her dress.

*   *   *

The cat was out on the deck the next morning. She was repeatedly climbing one of the square wooden columns that led straight up into the middle of an inaccessible beam.

101

Over and over again she scrambled her way up, realized she was going nowhere, and scraped herself back down. I watched her procedural dance and sipped my coffee. I should have named her Sisyphus.

Julia slid open the glass door behind me and stepped out onto the deck. She was swallowed in a loosely buttoned shirt of mine, pilfered from my closet. And nothing else. She'd brought a bag of her own clothes with her that I now realized had been accidentally left in the cab of my truck in our hurry to get indoors last night. She blew at her own cup of coffee and smirked at me.

"Who's cliché now?" I asked, tilting my head for a new kind of view.

"You get up too early," she pouted, taking the chair next to me.

"It's eight."

"It's Sunday."

"Patricia's not up yet," I pointed out, and ran a finger up her thigh. She pushed my hand off and stood up and put her coffee down. Swaying out to the far ledge, she settling her elbows on it with her back to me.

"She's going to make us go to brunch with her, isn't she," Julia feigned lamentation, arching her back as she stroked a hand through her hair. When she did that the shirt rode up higher.

"She will," I agreed, looking at her profiled against the wilderness. I sipped my coffee.

"Come here," she said softly.

I stood up and walked over and eased into her. A breeze touched our skin and my mind reeled as I got away with something and died inside all at the same time, again and again.

*   *   *

"Brunch dearies! Brunch time!" Patricia trumpeted across the yard an hour later. She was speeding towards us, purse swinging, sunhat steadied by French-manicured nail tips. Julia lounged next to me. She'd retrieved her bag from the truck and rejuvenated herself into a person wholly different but just as glowing. She wore slacks and a relaxed white button-down blouse, hair pulled back and secured in a lazy bun. She hadn't said much. Patricia's imminent arrival had been an easy excuse to make the last half hour a little less awkward. Necessity was the mother of invented ease.

"What a fantastic dress, Patricia," Julia beamed up at her as Pat climbed the steps and emanated impatience.

"Oh! Well, thank you, dear. So where are we off to?" She rooted around for something in her purse and suddenly threw a set of car keys at me. I caught them with my left hand, frowning.

"Julia and I are going to have lots of mimosas, Johnny, and your truck's just so...cramped, for three," Patricia explained. "It's a very nice Buick. Plenty of room for everyone. Julia can even have shotgun, you know I've never actually ridden in the back seat of my car, you'll be like my chauffeur! C'mon, I have to tell Silas where we're going, don't want to be y'alls third wheel for goodness sake. I'm paying!" She smiled from one of us to the other like she was trying to form us into a single amorphous love collective. My coffee suddenly tasted stale.

I waved idly at Leroy McGuff as I steered Patricia's boat-like sedan out onto the cul-de-sac, left foot ghosting for a clutch that wasn't there. Leroy was smoking a cigarette, and watering his roses. From beside and behind me, Julia and Patricia argued about where to eat in high-pitched voices. Finally they settled on Timber Grill, which was right down the road. Silas Giles lived right down the road, too. I was beginning to think that everything was right down the goddamn road. Patricia hit a few buttons on her cell phone and quickly engaged the detective with her phone voice.

Ten minutes later we were being seated in the bar area. ("The drinks come quicker if you sit in this room," Patricia explained.) A squirrelly-looking host was ducking his eyes and directing an out-of-uniform Silas Giles to our table from the front door. Giles strode over and slid in next to Patricia, who seemed to be more pleased at the impromptu double date than any of the rest of us.

"Isn't this fun," Patricia gushed. In her frenzy to avoid direct sunlight she immediately tangled herself in the window shade cord. Julia leaned across, freeing Pat and remedying the blinds. They both ordered mimosas between fits of celebratory giggles. Giles leaned back in the booth and crossed his arms, staying well out of the way. I followed suit.

"So, Giles dear, tell me about the Meers suicide," Patricia asked as soon as we'd ordered our food. I nearly choked on my orange juice.

The detective shot a glance up to Julia and me as though logging his audience in the file room of his head.

"What do you mean?" he asked, finally resting his gaze on Patricia.

"I mean what convinced y'all that it was a suicide? You know, what did you find, what did it prove?" Patricia asked. She plucked an orange wedge from the edge of her goblet and nibbled it with wide eyes, like she was just making small talk. Her earrings dangled like hypnotic traps for unsuspecting men.

"Uh, yeah," Giles paused, clearing his throat. "Well, we didn't find a suicide note or anything, but you don't always. She was on the couch. Gun in her left hand, we confirmed she was left-handed. Her and her husband's fingerprints on it, but it was his gun, which we knew." He stopped to blow a little at his hot coffee, returning it to the table without drinking.

"She was a prescription pill abuser," he continued, "and had always been a little depressed. The husband came home and found her, and he alibied out, but we tested his hands for gunshot residue anyway. He was clean. It was pretty clear cut." He paused. "At the time."

"But things have changed," Patricia pushed, twirling an unused straw around her drink.

"Well, when he went missing, we searched his house," Giles admitted. "There was that blackmail note y'all got your hands on. No one showed from either end at the pickup site. And in the house we found some things. Like gloves...with gunshot residue. Besides which, we did an autopsy. Didn't tell the press at the time, but she was pregnant. We just want to ask him some questions."

"What was Dillon Meers' alibi?" Julia spoke up beside me in full reporter mode.

"Well it was a Saturday, and he'd left in the morning to go hang out with a friend of his, and the friend confirmed they were together the whole day. Partaking of some questionable substances, but together nonetheless," explained the detective.

"Who was the friend?" Julia asked aloud, as Patricia asked with her eyes.

Giles glanced at me. "Local dealer by the name of Zebulon Fix," he said finally.

That time I did choke. Julia patted me on the back. A plump waitress approached with a large tray, doling out our food and mumbling about hash browns. Jason Controy and his parents walked in. Patricia drowned the waitress out with exuberant salutations to the Controys. I nodded numbly at them and tried to hear anything in my head other than Zebulon Fix saying *"I'll see if I can't return the favor sometime."*

*　　　*　　　*

"Dear Johnny," it started, and I immediately wanted to rip it to pieces and save myself from reading it. Em had stood up our lunch dates all week that December. I hadn't seen her for five days. I thought I'd done something wrong, but then I reached the more horrifying conclusion that I hadn't.

Dear Johnny,

You helped me. But you don't belong in the dark like I do. You are my sunlit sin; surprising, addictive. You were the only thing that almost saved me. But it's all nothing and always has been, after all.

I'm pregnant with our child, which of course I cannot be. My realities aren't mixing well anymore. Nothing ever does.

I want you to know that I loved you. Intensely—more than I thought I could. I thought love might save me, but it didn't. I think I wasn't designed to be happy. I don't even know what people mean when they talk about the word; aren't we always usually cold and hungry and hurt and desperate, even when we're together? Once, I thought I was happy when I was twelve, I remember the feeling—there was sun and rain and baseball and a cute boy that grinned at me. I felt that feeling every once in awhile with you. Which isn't enough. I'm sorry I let you down.

The moon has been shining full on snow this month, and the blue brightness outside in the early morning is refreshing. Moonlight is more honest than sunlight, I think. I got so distracted by us in sunlight.

I'm going back to what I was meant for. I'm sorry you met me as I am. Like I always told you—you were too late. By no fault of your own, my love. Don't think twice—it's alright.

Forever,

Darby

And so, pregnant with our child, she left me.

It took me two hours too many to realize the breakup letter she'd slipped under my apartment door in the early morning was a suicide note. I was too busy feeling sorry for myself. When I started driving, it wasn't fast enough. When I found her, it wasn't soon enough. I'd long since researched her address, although I'd never been there. But I sped there as dawn was breaking. The GPS voice was automating my route in a way that made me want to punch through the metal of my truck. I finally got there, somehow. I pulled straight into the driveway and slammed my brakes next to her green Jeep. The front door was unlocked. I knew it would be. I went in and I took only two steps, until I saw.

I saw Darby Meers. The girl I called Em, because it made her smile. The girl I would have died for. And she was dead. I saw the blood, crimson turned dark to mock my lateness. I saw that little pistol I taught her how to shoot, half fallen out of her limp hand. I backed out. I closed the door. I pulled out of the driveway. I noticed the rhododendrons lining my retreat, because they were Em's favorite plant. I noticed the woods, because they were Em's favorite setting. I saw the mountains, distant and immovable, because they were Em's favorite sight. I remembered the cold, handwritten pregnancy announcement, because I felt like all of me had died. I remembered the blood dripping down her face, but it wasn't from her nose this time.

And I noticed the "For Sale" sign next to the driveway of the little A-frame next door.

*   *   *

"You okay, Jep?" Julia was patting me on the back as

the eggs in front of me approached room temperature.

"Oh," I paused to gulp some juice, "Just fine. Just rethinking some things. Weird case."

"I think Mr. Jepko has perhaps made acquaintance with Mr. Fix," Detective Giles said helpfully from across the table, relieved to not be the center of attention.

"Johnny! Why do I not know this!" Patricia nearly shouted at me.

"I hadn't been made aware of his full relevance to 'your' case, Pat," I tried to say calmly, eying the detective. He wasn't looking in my direction. He didn't plan to.

I dug into my eggs and thought about how unreliable an alibi from Zebulon Fix probably was. And how I missed running my fingers down Darby's sides, right along her rib cage. I never was too good at dealing with death happening right in front of me—not ever. I shoveled another mouthful of eggs in my mouth and looked out of the window at the West Virginia mountains. They were coated in green forests and just big enough to make men feel small.

THIRTEEN

The way the newspapers announced her death was like this:

> *Darby Anne Meers, 29, of Elmcroft, formerly of Charleston, died after a brief illness last Friday. She is survived by her husband, Dillon Meers, and parents, Phillip and Charlene Lotts of Charleston.*

I figured the gunshot had been brief but the illness probably wasn't.

I put a bid in on the house next door to hers the day after I read her obituary. I didn't know why, but the compulsion ate through my numbness, so I welcomed it.

*   *   *

Zebulon Fix showed up on my deck the next day with West Virginia Power tickets and questionable intentions. I wondered what I would owe him if I accepted his invitation to the ball game.

"To what do I owe this honor," I asked. I tried to lean around him to get an idea if he was carrying or not. His clothes were far more clandestine today, more black than yellow in team colors. The tickets, on the other hand, were right in my face.

"Hey, man, you were good enough to tell me bout them plants, and frankly, my girl ducked out on me last night, don't wanna see 'em go to waste. Game's at seven, we're playin' Lexington," he said, like that explained his sudden generosity.

"Well it's...very nice of you," I said, removing my glasses to wipe humidity off my forehead. My evening was shot, anyway. A Monday afternoon of lots of work and lots of clients that didn't want to pay for it had exhausted me to the point of lethargy. Plus, I didn't think Zebulon Fix would shoot me at a minor league baseball stadium. I told him to give me a minute to change clothes, and accepted.

"I'll drive separately though—gotta pick up some groceries on the way back," I lied.

"Sure thing boss. You got my number. Meet you in the parking garage." Zeb said easily.

I had no idea what he was up to. He didn't seem like the type that was low on friends.

He waited until I grabbed my wallet and phone and headed out to his beat up Honda, pulling out of the driveway in front of me. I followed him out of the subdivision and down the road to the I-79 entrance ramp. The two of us sped separately towards Appalachian Power Park. I hadn't been to a game since before my dad had died, but I figured Fix would make for more talkative company anyway. I was somewhat interested in what he would have to say.

After a handful of miles my phone rang through my car speakers via Bluetooth and voodoo. I momentarily faltered trying to locate the answer button, which was suspiciously built into my steering wheel. I finally did, swerving only slightly.

"Yeah?" I shouted to the dashboard.

"Guess who I passed coming in as I was leaving our road, dear," Patricia's voice crackled through the speakers.

"Zebulon Fix," I yelled.

"Stop yelling, Johnny! And how did you know that!"

"He came to take me out to the ole ballgame. Weird, huh?" I continued to shout over the road noise she couldn't hear.

"And you're going? He's a drug dealer, Johnny!"

If I squinted I could see her standing in her kitchen with a hand on her hips.

"Right! I promise not to buy any. Gotta go, pulling in." I wrenched the wheel. "Bye Patricia!" I yelled.

I listened to several seconds more of chiding before I punched the hang-up button.

Zeb stretched out of his car several spots down from me. He didn't say much as we walked across to the stadium. We each procured a beer and chili dog from the concessions, and found our seats just a couple rows above the Power's dugout.

"Nice seats," I complimented, leaning back.

"Only the best," he said, chortling once and taking an extended swig of beer.

I sucked my elbow in from the aisle as a careening toddler attempted to trip his way into a wipeout on the steps. He slammed into the arms of paternal instincts several rows down. I shrugged off the guilt of not catching him myself. Once I had almost been a father, just as unseen winds sometimes douse tiny sparks before they grow into raging fires. Zeb asked what I thought about the new shortstop and I took a swig of cold beer.

The next few hours went by faster than I expected. I

eventually began to feel at home among the cracks of ball to bat and the intermittent heckling from Rowdy Alley and rowdier fans. The air cooled as the stadium lights took over for the sinking sun. I could still make out the capitol dome blocks away in the East End, shining away serenely. It winked at me once.

It was a nice night. A relaxing night. And my degenerate companion was turning out to be a good conversationalist and a discerning baseball fan. We talked about hotdog chili and the good old days at Watt Powell Park, and debated historically great relief pitchers and team chemistry and the superiority of Charleston's minor league. The Power won, sneaking in an RBI double in the bottom of the eighth and staving off the Legends in the end.

"So they found Meers yet?" Zeb asked in a casual tone as we made our way back to our cars.

Right, of course. Maybe it was the raucous still of the night game that had dulled my curiosity about Zeb's ulterior motives. Or the stomachful of draft beer.

"Nope," I answered, shoving my hands in my pockets. "Reopened his wife's case, though. Think he might have killed her, made it look like a suicide or something, and someone was on to him, was blackmailing him, and he ran."

"Is that so," Zeb said calmly, seeming to consider the information. "Well," he pulled a can of Skoal from a pocket and rapped it against his palm. "He is kind of a dick."

"I thought you two were friends," I said, glancing over at him. I tried not to sound too curious.

He finished stuffing a pinch of tobacco beneath his lip before he answered. "More like business associates, boss. He owes me some money."

"Didn't you, uh...alibi him out, though?" I asked carefully.

"Oh, sure. I'm in the business of favors. Among

other things," he grinned. The dip protruded his bottom lip in a way that made him look a little bit maniacal.

"So he wasn't really with you that day," I half-asked, half-stated. I kept my gaze straight ahead.

"Well who's to say, boss? 'Sides, I wouldn't want to get myself in the unfortunate predicament of bein' thought a blackmailer, would I," he grinned again.

"Ah, right," I agreed, deciding promptly to drop the topic. We were almost at our vehicles, anyway. "Thanks again for the ticket," I said, "Great game."

"Sure," Zeb nodded, "Thanks for comin'-with. Hey now, you let me know if they come up with anything new with Meers, won't ya?" He opened his car door.

"Will do," I said, unlocking my truck. Maybe Zeb didn't have a lot of friends, after all. Anybody that used people like he did didn't strike me as a good candidate for forging a lot of strong relationships. I was happy to be used, though. It suited my purposes just fine.

*   *   *

By the time I pulled onto Talon Creek Road it was finally full dark. The truck's glowing clock only said 9:30, and I realized it had been a short game, as games go. Dire Straits was serenading sultans on my radio but the signal was sputtering out. I was just about to flick the sound off when my headlights caught shiny blackness in the cul-de-sac. There was water seeping across the pavement from the slight bank of Leroy McGuff's yard. It was strange and snaking about on the otherwise bone-dry asphalt. The only thing my headlights caught in his yard was the row of rose bushes. I slowed down, surprised he wasn't standing amongst them with his garden hose, creating the rivulets. Of course, I might have been just as surprised to see him watering in the dark, much less aiming his hose at the road. A mild uneasiness started in my stomach. Or maybe it was already there, and I just became aware of it.

I eased the truck over the streams of water like they were speed bumps, and drove on up my driveway. I parked and reached behind me to get the big Maglite I kept in the cab. I looked across my deck at Patricia's house but all the lights were out, which was unusual for her this early. I took off back down the driveway on foot, flashlight in hand. Neither the moon nor its effects were anywhere to be seen. I navigated along the gravel, thinking I might check my mail, but that could wait. I walked on over to the mini-streams I'd noticed, and followed them to the edge of McGuff's yard, calling out. The night was still, except for the gurgling liquid. I sidestepped the wetness, waving the flashlight around. I continued on up the yard, beam now trained on the liquid darkness running through the grass. The lights in the house were out, but his car was in the driveway. I knew his wife worked late at a beauty salon, but I hadn't thought she worked *this* late.

I could hear the hose now, spewing against clumpy resistant grass. The water led right up to the row of rose bushes, and I could just see the black plastic of the nozzle. It was locked on, topping the sea green hose that protruded from under a bush. Next to it lay a motionless hand, palm up. I called out again to Leroy. The hand didn't move, but the dogs started a series of growls and yaps from the backyard.

I froze for a second, processing, or trying to process. Then I shoved forward between bushes, scratching my hands on thorns, and swinging the flashlight beam to the side. I took a step back and froze again. Leroy McGuff was lying half on his side, arm extending from underneath him. His eyes were open, or at least, one was. I couldn't see the other one. It was obscured by blood from where his head had been bashed in.

I kneeled down to check his pulse even though I knew there wouldn't be one. I knew what dried blood looked like. I tried standing, but my knees reeled and I thought better of it. I leaned a hand on the ground somewhere away from blood and water and peeled my cell phone from my pocket with the other hand. I bowed my head for a minute to stop myself from screaming, or vomiting, or both. Righting myself, I dialed 9-1-1. I engaged with the dispatcher just as the headlights of Jolene McGuff's sedan lit up the trees along the road. They glared full force into my eyes as she swung into the McGuff driveway.

"110 Talon Creek Road," I continued, getting up and taking off towards her at a run. My knees forgot to waver. "He's dead. Hit in the head. Hard."

I caught Jolene in the midriff with my right arm as she stumbled out of her still-running car. My left arm kept the cell phone glued to my ear. Her swinging headlights had betrayed her, showed her things she wasn't ready to see. Would never be ready to see. As soon as she ran into my arm she collapsed, her will betraying her strength.

"Don't go over there," was all I could think to say to Jolene as I restrained her. She already knew. She wasn't fighting me anyway; her soul was busy fighting the universe.

"Please hurry," I said to the dispatcher. I didn't think the operator could hear me anymore over the guttural screams of the widow crumpling to the grass through my embrace. I wondered if sudden grief looked the same on everybody.

FOURTEEN

When I was young, I asked my dad what a cul-de-sac was. I'd heard the word on television during an advertisement for my mother's favorite daytime soap opera.

"A goddamned dead end," he had grumbled, like the word itself offended him. Most things offended him. People did; ideas did. Gourmet food definitely did, and you didn't want to get him started in on sound poetry.

Ten years later he was busy screaming to a customer service representative whom he believed responsible for cancelling that daytime soap opera, and had a stroke. He died that afternoon. Mom never did get her show back. I remember the sounds she made when she found him, though.

*   *   *

I looked up to see a fire truck entering the cul-de-sac, pulling in beside the bank of McGuff's yard. Was there a fire, too? I wouldn't have noticed. I didn't hear the sirens coming because they blended in with Jolene's shrieks and the dog howls and the panic in my brain. I saw the red of the truck, though. I watched two alien figures get out and run up the driveway. Then I saw a freakishly large ambulance pull into the driveway itself. Had emergency vehicles always been so big? Were fire trucks always so red? Where had I dropped my phone, with the calm instructions of that 9-1-1 dispatcher? Was it somewhere here in the grass where Jolene was screaming?

Now the bright emergency vehicle lights lit up the yard as two more aliens jumped from the ambulance. The first paramedic jogged forward to carefully measure a soul. I could see him now, in the lights. He was human. He was an ally. He reached down to Leroy's carotid and after several seconds shook his head at his compatriots, who were standing yards away in the driveway, holding a stretcher. He had seen what I had—skin too purple and brain too exposed to warrant resuscitation. They all retreated as detective-bearing cruisers arrived. Vehicles clogged the driveway, spilling out into the damp cul-de-sac. Nobody had turned the hose off. The pair of EMTs seemed disappointed, maybe because a man was dead, and they had no one to save. I wanted to raise my hand to volunteer. The other paramedic from the ambulance was already with us. He'd been trying to pry Jolene McGuff out of my arms the whole time.

*   *   *

Patricia was awoken by the general chaos. I saw her ducking through shadows on her way across the road to reach us. The Controys emerged soon after. A pajama-laden Kim turned to shoo Jason back down towards the darkness of their house.

"What's happening?" Patricia whispered fiercely as

she approached. Giles was midway through my interrogation, and I couldn't tell which one of us she was asking. She was hugging a silky looking dark green robe around her. She seethed efficiency, despite mussed hair and sleep-drugged eyes. David and Jo Controy were standing at the foot of the McGuff driveway, hovering in ill-lit indecision.

"Everyone go back home," Giles ordered. He leaned over his shoulder and glanced sharply at the police deputies struggling to erect crime scene tape. Patricia peered toward the rose bushes and the small group of people on the other side. She spied Jolene McGuff, wrapped in a blanket and leaning on the side of a vehicle with a deputy's hand steadying her shoulder.

"Is Leroy dead, Silas," Patricia asked in a weirdly chiding tone.

"He is," Giles said, "And I need you to go back home, talk to no one, and make some coffee. We'll be over soon to speak with you."

I was surprised to see her do as she was told. The Controys followed suit. Patricia gave me a parting glance of sympathy. I probably still had a look of horror on my face.

"You were out at a baseball game with *who?*" Giles continued our conversation.

"With Zeb Fix," I said, and hoped he wouldn't ask why.

"When did the game start?" Giles asked. A brief flash in his eyes belied his disapproval at the company I'd been keeping, but he made no comment. He stayed stern and calm, and asked me the usual questions, in the usual way.

"Tent...TENT!" Giles yelled suddenly. Officers juggling tape, stakes, kits, and cameras stopped, and searched starless skies.

I looked up. A single raindrop hit and rolled off my spherical eyeglass lens. Then it started to pour.

There was a scramble. I didn't remember any rain being forecast, and apparently neither did anyone else. Somebody found a tarp in one of the cruisers. The actual forensic people were only just setting up. Four deputies elevated corners of plastic over and between inconveniently placed rose bushes. They were tippy-toe in the increasing sludge. I always knew those roses' days were numbered.

I was relieved from my interrogation by Giles' sudden deluge of responsibilities. I walked back to my house through the highlighted flashes of emergency lights. I had recovered my cell phone, but I had no idea where my Maglite was. I'd lost it too long ago to care. It was pushing midnight. As he'd let me go Giles had promised that we'd reconvene for the rest of the interview that evening. My deck lights were on, and I breathed a sigh, intent on making coffee. But instead I found Patricia, with a thermos and two coffee cups. She gestured to me to hurry, as if I'd taken too long.

"Here Johnny, I didn't have any sugar, so I'm gonna top it with a little whip cream. I usually drink it black but I think we could use something sweet," she explained, talking in a rush and forcing the can to exhale on my cup and hers. I took mine gratefully, and she leaned back in a coil spring chair, green robe weirdly brilliant. The rain pounded the roof above us and the ground beyond us.

I waited for her to ask me a lot of questions. She didn't. I waited for the coffee to cool instead, and took a sip.

"Fuck," I said.

"Well it's Irish Coffee, John," Patricia looked over seriously. Nobody ambushed like Patricia Murgatroyd.

"You're mad at me for going out with Fix," I guessed.

"Well yes, but no, dear, you found our neighbor dead tonight. I thought you might need an...enhanced coffee."

"I do not," I groaned.

"I brought another batch," she said with great disappointment. Sure enough, she grabbed a second thermos from below her feet. She set it on the table in front of me. I splashed my Irish coffee over the edge of the deck to join the rain, which made Patricia cringe. I got a refill from the new thermos, then I leaned back and told her everything—game, streaming water, blood, and screaming.

It wasn't raining anymore. A light wind blew leftover raindrops off thousands of leaves. The effect was almost the same as a light sprinkle. All around us, secondhand raindrops plinked and plopped. Like things needed more moisture around here.

"I have something to show you tomorrow," Patricia was saying. Headlights bounced up my driveway and a deputy arrived with Detective Giles. I wondered why they hadn't just walked.

"Is Pat here?" He boomed from the driveway, flashlight trying to blind me. The corner of my house blocked his view of Patricia.

"I'm here, Silas," Patricia said calmly, but loud enough to be heard over latent raindrops.

"I told you to go home," Giles said roughly, stepping onto the deck and jerking back the plastic hood of a yellow poncho. I suspected he was as relieved as he was angry. He cleared his face in an instant and motioned the deputy in the driveway to join him. This was the same woman who had asked why I was wearing a tie the last time I met her. How fortunate that I had changed into a t-shirt for the ballgame.

"We've managed to confirm you called 9-1-1 before Mrs. McGuff showed up, and that she was at her salon late tonight," Giles started in, "and we're trying to contact Mr. Fix, but can't seem to get a hold of him yet. Do you know where he was going after the game?"

"No clue," I said, "but he had mentioned he had just broken up with a girlfriend and that's why he had the tickets available, I think." The female deputy had pulled a pen and pad from a small bag over her shoulder. She was scribbling furiously. I noticed her name tag for the first time; it read "ASHLEY." I zoned out a little, realizing that was her last name, not her first.

"And one more thing," the detective said evenly. He motioned to Deputy Ashley, who ceased writing and leaned a hand into the small duffle bag.

"Is this yours?" Giles asked me. The deputy had stepped forward to dangle an evidence bag in front of my face. In it was my flashlight. It had obviously been wet when it was put in the bag, and the wetness had smeared off onto the clear plastic. The streaks were red.

"Yes," I said after a second, "I must have dropped it beside him when I checked for a pulse, I guess it got his blood on it from the ground."

"That's what we figured," Giles said slowly. "Still, best if you come down to the station with us tonight. To give a full statement."

"O-kay," I said with equal sluggishness.

"Now that's just ridiculous, Silas," Patricia piped up beside me, "You know Johnny, he obviously had nothing to do with this, just happened to find the body! Surely he can get a good night's sleep and wait til morning to—"

I turned to her. "It's fine, Pat."

"Well," Patricia huffed.

Giles' cell rang and he answered quickly, moving away a few steps and turning his back to us. He spoke low monosyllables into the receiver, doing more listening than talking. I stared at Deputy Ashley, who stared back, jutting her chin out beneath sleepy eyes. Her hair was in a ponytail, but the humidity had frizzed it out around her face in a backlit halo. After a few moments Giles turned back around to us.

"Do you own a shovel?" he asked me.

"Uh, yeah," I said, "right over in the corner there with the rake and things." I twisted and gestured to the far corner of my deck. A haphazard pile of tools leaned up against the wood siding of my house.

"Show me," Giles said, already striding forward.

I got up and joined him, clearing my throat and indicating the square point shovel. He reached in with gloved hands and retrieved it from behind a scrub broom. He lifted it up horizontally and held it under the lights, running his eyes along its length.

"What's this—concrete?" He waved a finger at white residue on the front of the blade.

"Yeah, actually," I said, pointing to the deck in front of my sliding glass doors. "Installed a little concrete stoop down there when I moved in before I realized I wanted something a little...bigger." I rolled my eyes up and around the expanse of the 600-square-foot covered deck.

"Don't blame you," Giles said. He flipped the shovel over. More concrete residue on the back side of the blade. I couldn't tell if he was surprised at the absence of blood.

"May we take this, just to test," he asked casually, as if he weren't suggesting that I'd murdered my neighbor.

"Sure," I said.

"Honestly, Silas!" Patricia spoke up again, cinching up her robe for a look of offended royalty. "You cannot think that's a murder weapon! And if he was killed by a shovel, well, everyone around here owns a shovel! Why—"

"Speaking of which, we'll be needing your shovel too, Patricia, " he said evenly. "The initial report is that he died several hours before he was found. Any shovel in the area could have been used and returned, not necessarily by its owner. Or taken away and hidden or disposed of elsewhere. We just need to eliminate possibilities." He stopped, almost sighing. I could tell he didn't like to explain so much. Patricia seemed to guess this, and made an effort to relax herself.

"Very well," she said, "I'll go get it."

"I'll come with you. I don't want you handling it," Giles said before she could protest. "Deputy Ashley, please stay here with Mr. Jepko."

Patricia pressed her lips together and followed him off the deck towards her house.

I walked over to the far edge of my deck and looked out. I took a deep breath, catching the vague sweetness of nearby honeysuckle vines. The vines were touting their wares to an aeonian collection of nighttime moths. I heard the distant palpation of bullfrogs, and the closer dripping of trees. I shuddered slightly at the thought of my fallen flashlight on bloody grass. I turned my palms up and studied them.

"What are you doin'?" The deputy behind me asked immediately.

"Looking for blood, I don't know," I said. "I touched him."

"Why?" she barked.

"When I took his pulse. To see if he was dead. Or due diligence, or something." She didn't respond, but I could still feel her looking at me.

Patricia and Giles returned quietly and the detective cleared his throat.

"That'll be all for tonight folks," he said, "Why don't both of you come down to the station first thing tomorrow morning."

"Okay," I said. I was surprised at the prospect of sleeping.

"Let's go, Ashley," he said gruffly to the deputy. She re-shouldered her duffle bag and followed him out to the cruiser. Patricia poured herself a drink from the spiked thermos and sat silently back in her seat, still enrobed. I watched the police pull out and realized the headlights weren't headed back across the street. They were making a wide rightward U-turn into Dillon Meer's driveway. The officers pulled nearly all the way down the driveway, and got out of the car with the headlights still on. The beams of two flashlights blinked to life and started to bob around his house.

I looked back at the still-silent Patricia, whose eyes were slightly wider than they had been before.

"Are you okay?" I asked.

"Not really, Johnny." She took a sip from her mug without meeting my gaze. "My shovel is missing."

FIFTEEN

When I was an undergrad at the University of Virginia, I used to wander around the campus lawn with a pocket-size Nikon strapped to my neck. I took endless photographs of the Jeffersonian architecture for which the area was known. On the weekends I'd drive up to Washington, DC, less than three hours away. There I'd take more shots of the capital's buildings and the weird black squirrels that populated the green city lawns. The squirrels all came in gray where I was from.

A bike cop outside the White House fence stopped me once. I'd just taken a photo of him and several of his peers chatting in a semicircle. They were half-astride bicycles, adorned in white polos and black helmets.

"Let me see that camera," the cop ordered as I started to move away. He was in his fifties, a big man but not fat. His head was full of thick silver hair and his expression was unreadable.

My heart jumped around and landed in my stomach

like it did every time I drew police attention. It was reticent guilt from a misspent youth, wherein I had occasionally found myself running from the sites of minor misdemeanors.

"Here you go, sir," I said quickly, pulling the photo up on the little LCD screen.

"Hmm," he frowned at the picture as he studied it. Then he handed me back the camera.

"I've been trying to tell them I'm the tallest," he said as he turned away.

*   *   *

I drove us to the county Sheriff's the next morning in Patricia's Buick. We were seated for a few minutes in the waiting area before Detective Giles came out to greet us.

"Thank you for coming in," he said, his tone formal. "Mr. Jepko, you can come with me, and Patricia, another officer will be out to meet you shortly."

Patricia looked visibly hurt at being passed off. Giles was distancing himself from us, and especially Pat, as fast as he could. Homicide detectives dating suspects was frowned upon, I guessed.

My interview was mostly redundant, but I went into more detail, making things a little clearer. Giles asked a few extra questions which I answered easily. Just when I thought we were through, he asked me something I wasn't expecting.

"Did you say Zebulon Fix had broken up with his girlfriend?" He leaned back, gaze level.

"I think so, yes...or, he was explaining why he happened to have two tickets to the game and said it was because his girl had 'run out on him' or something, I assumed that's what he meant."

"I see," Giles said.

"Not the case?" I tried to sound subtle.

"Just a strange thing to say for someone who we finally located at his girlfriend's house," Giles said. I wondered if anything Fix had ever said to me was truthful.

I was excused after volunteering prints and swabs to an eager young lab tech. I emerged just in time to hear Patricia's high pitched protestations against "any such thing."

"I resent your implications, young man!" She was clutching her purse to her chest as if she were addressing a street thief. "Why, what if I want to commit some magnificent crime some day! What then! I certainly do not give you permission to swab me! To have my body on file! How vulgar!"

Giles came up behind me, audibly sighing.

The young deputy in front of Pat had his head cocked, one eyebrow raised over a mouth that was a couple ticks away from a sneer. "Ma'am," he managed to get out without too much derision, "You mean you won't give us DNA because you might commit a *future* crime?"

"Well what," Pat said, splaying sarcastic hands at him, "Are you going to start up a Kanawha pre-crime unit right there in the file room? I saw the movie young man, Tommy was just brilliant! Now, unless I am under arrest, we will be leaving!" She blinked finally at him and headed towards me, linking her elbow in mine and ignoring Detective Giles. The detective had opened his mouth as if to say something, but then closed it. I shrugged in his direction and escorted the lady to her Buick.

Several miles from home she indicated that I should stop at a sports bar for an early lunch. It was a foregone conclusion that her early lunch would be mostly liquid. Her performance this morning had been sober, so I supposed she needed to make up for lost time. I pulled her big white sedan in at the end of a line of motorcycles. The front of the one-story building was flat, windowless, and identified only by its crooked vinyl banner. Pat walked straight to the door and threw it open.

"Well, if it's not Patricia Murgatroyd!" a grizzled man behind the bar blared as we entered. I adjusted my eyes to the dark interior. Several bikers on bar stools turned and joined in with choruses of "Hey, Patsy." What the fuck else had I expected?

"Darts later, boys," she said quickly, leaning an elbow in on the bar between two of them. "Jim, I need a bucket of Budlight and a couple menus out on the deck, dear. Thanks so much. Would you believe I've spent my morning being harassed by the police!" She addressed this to the room at large, and several of the men chuckled.

"You back into that 'shine again?" one asked, his girth making his bar stool look spindly.

"I reckon she finally killed somebody," a pair of lips muttered from underneath a trucker hat.

"Of course not," Patricia snapped. She accepted a bucket full of ice and bottles from the bartender and shoved it in my direction. I grabbed it and she took my elbow, leading me to a small door towards the back. To my surprise, it opened up to a finely built deck looking out over the Elk River.

"He's a li'l young for ya, eh Patsy?" said a voice from inside as the door thudded shut behind us.

"Here we go, Johnny," Pat said, placing the bucket in the middle of a round table close to the rail. I sat, taking in the view. A slight breeze whispered past my skin and suddenly the tension and trauma from the previous 24 hours lessened. I suspected that Patricia had foreseen this.

"Nice," I said.

"You don't think yours is the only deck I frequent, do you dear?" Patricia smiled, grabbing a bottle of beer and holding it out to me to open.

"My nails," she explained, rubbing a thumb over blue manicured digits.

"You really switch up the alcohol, huh? I mean, you don't have a favorite drink? Even...type of drink, that you prefer?" I asked, twisting the beer open and handing it back.

"Why would I limit myself like that?" She looked at me as if the concept was confusing.

"Nevermind," I said, adjusting my glasses. A slim waitress slipped outside through a server door, bringing two menus.

"Well," Patricia said after the girl had left, "I know who did it."

"Who killed Leroy, you mean?"

"Of course that's what I mean, Johnny!"

"Oh, so...you didn't kill him?"

Patricia rolled her eyes.

"Well who?" I raised an eyebrow.

Patricia daintily lifted her beer as she paused to look out over the wide flatness of Elk River. I followed her eyes. The water mirrored the sky and the trees on the opposite bank almost perfectly. This far up you couldn't see ripples. Though it had a feeling of depth, from here the river looked like a sheet of glass.

Patricia turned back and sipped from her beer, whetting my anticipation.

"Dillon Meers," she finally announced.

"I thought you thought he was dead," I said.

"Not anymore. I don't think he ever left the area. Just think, Johnny—we saw them going over to search his house again last night. Probably looking for evidence that he's been there! And let's say he HAD been—and Leroy McGuff saw him! Dillon Meers wants the world to think he's dead. So if someone saw him…"

"He'd have to kill them?" I asked.

"Exactly." Patricia nodded curtly.

"I think you might be missing something," I told her.

"What? What?" her eyes widened.

"Loathe as I am to admit this, remember your original theory that Leroy was the one blackmailing Meers?"

"Oh! My! God!" She put a hand to her chest.

"—which would give Meers a pretty good reason to kill him," I thought Patricia was going to clap her hands in glee.

"I FORGOT about our blackmail note!" she shrieked at me.

"Yep," I agreed.

My stomach suddenly plummeted and I felt wrenched with guilt. I had known Leroy, not really well, but well enough. He didn't deserve to be called a blackmailer, even posthumously. That was Pat's shtick.

The waitress came out to take our orders.

"So, Johnny," Patricia said after we'd asked for sub sandwiches, "Like I was saying last night, I have somewhere I want to show you."

"You said what last night?" I looked up.

"On your deck, with the coffee, before—nevermind," she gulped at her beer, "I have somewhere I want to show you," she repeated.

"Well...okay," I said, opening a beer of my own, "Where?"

"I'm not going to *tell* you," she said, as if I'd affronted her.

"Then...when?" I tried.

"When are you free, dear?" She asked, sounding secretarial.

"Well, since this morning is blown, I guess I need to put some work in after we get back, and I have a—"

"Excellent, tomorrow it is, then," she proclaimed, looking pleased.

"Okay, whatever." I took a sip of beer. "How long will this take?"

"Not so long, not so long. Meet you on your deck at ten?"

"Sure," I said. I found it strange that Patricia was pre-announcing a time she would be on my deck. I had about a 50/50 chance of her being on my deck already every time I walked out of my goddamn door.

The waitress arrived with our food and we ate in relative peace. I knew better than to ask Pat questions about something she clearly wanted to keep a mystery. If she planned on surprising me with a visit to a nail salon and smoothies at the Town Center Mall, though, I planned on surprising her by installing locking doors in my open deck entryways. But I trusted her. Despite her innate desire to constantly intoxicate me, I was sure she wouldn't take things too far. Or at least, I was pretty sure.

After drinking four of our six bottles she left me with the bill, and told me she'd be inside. I waited for the waitress to come back. I caught a whiff of cigarette smoke and turned to see the server standing slightly below and behind me at the side of the building. Her arms were crossed and her eyes were vacant as she took occasional puffs of a Camel. I stared at her for a few seconds and appreciated the fact that she wasn't playing on a cell phone. I preferred her old-school negligence.

I pocketed my wallet and went inside, where I asked Jim the bartender if I could settle the tab. He jovially acquiesced, took my credit card, and nodded over to the corner. "The girl's got it today!" he smiled at me.

The lunch crowd was in full swing now, and I looked over the row of baseball caps lining the bar. In the far corner, a small dart had just found the bullseye to the whoops of several bikers. Patricia had thrown it. I leaned my back up against the bar and studied what there was of decor. Take out the barflies and the place could have passed for a run-down antique shop. Patricia strutted over a few moments later, as the bartender was handing me back my card.

"Here," she said, trying to stuff something down my pants pocket.

"I got it, I got it!" I swatted her away, lifting the corner of the bill to see that it was a twenty. I look at her quizzically.

"For lunch, and driving. I never carry cash, you know," she explained.

"You just won this?"

"I won fifty, but you aren't worth that much, dear." I thought she was about to pinch my cheek.

"Alright, well, ready to head out?" I asked, but Patricia's gaze had left me for one of the widescreens behind the bar. It featured a local police press conference.

"...so we are asking once again for the public's help in locating Mr. Meers, who is now believed to still be in the area," the Police Chief was saying. "If sighted, please keep your distance and contact us immediately. He is considered armed and dangerous and is wanted for questioning in regard to several homicides—"

"Again," Julia Winfield's likeness suddenly flashed onto the screen, "that was Chief Tepper of Kanawha County, from the earlier press conference, reminding us to be on the lookout for Mr. Dillon Meers, pictured here, now wanted in connection to not one, but two possible murders," she paused, pressing a finger to one ear, "and we have finally heard from a police source that one of those homicides is that of Leroy McGuff, Jr., who was found dead last night in the yard of his Elmcroft home. We will be reporting more on that later, and keeping you up to date with this ongoing investigation throughout the day. This is Julia Winfield, thank you for watching W-K-A-N news."

Dillon Meer's photo took up the screen now, distorted by non-calibrated widescreen resolution. It looked like a mugshot, but I guess it had been pulled from his driver's license. His eyes were wide open but he looked like he had better things to do. He had a plain, unremarkable face, unimproved by a close-cropped haircut. It was grown out on top, with short, unmanaged bangs reflecting his general look of disregard.

Patricia punched me in the shoulder.

"Told you," she said.

SIXTEEN

The next morning I walked onto my deck in boxers, coffee in hand. It was about nine, and the mountains were still warming up. Sunshine chewed up the mist and the trees twinkled with orangey angled rays. Just as I leaned forward to blow some heat away from my mug, the cat, who I'd evidently left outside all night, leapt off the deck railing and charged. I watched dumbfounded as she galloped towards me. She swiveled into the air a few feet away, and attached herself to my bare lower leg, letting her claws sink in.

I yelled in pain and reflexively kicked her off, spilling hot coffee all over myself. The cat barrel-rolled across the wood before skidding herself to a halt a few yards away. She immediately jerked upright and began licking her side, not in pain, but casually. It was as if her mission had been accomplished and there was no more to be done except perhaps a nice self-cleansing prelude to basking in the sun.

"Fuck you," I spat, glancing down at my bloodied leg and stained boxers. She looked up, twitched an ear, and went back to licking herself. I doubt she was even hungry.

*   *   *

When Patricia arrived a little before ten I was dabbing antibiotic ointment onto my leg's scrapes and punctures as I tried to remember the last time I'd had a Tetanus booster. I'd re-showered, changed into a clean pair of boxers, and procured a spray bottle full of water. I sat it menacingly on the deck table in front of me. It was meant to intimidate the cat, who had her back to me, lolling in a sunray.

"Hello, kitten," Patricia cooed in a baby voice, walking up the steps in uncharacteristic jeans and tennis shoes. She reached down to scratch the calico fondly on the head, then rose back up, skin intact, before sauntering over to me. She raised her overly large sunglasses to get a better look.

"What in the world happened, Johnny!" she exclaimed, and then, letting her voice drop, "You get all dressed down for me, doll?" Her eyes roamed over my bare chest.

"Cut it out, Pat," I hissed, "That feral fucking fleabag just attacked me for no reason." I winced, accidentally pressing too hard on a claw mark.

"Oh not no reason, dear," Patricia paused, taking a seat, and glancing back at the cat. "She doesn't like you much."

"The fuck did I do to her," I growled.

"Animals can sense things, Johnny—"

"So where are we going?" I asked, cutting her off. "You're early."

"Well, yes, I am, I was thinking of inviting Sherry along, but she's been there before, plus when I called she already had plans, and I suppose three's a crowd after all," she answered unhelpfully.

"Well, sure, we just never get to spend time together," I said.

"What's that? Do you think we spend too much time with each other, Johnny?"

I crumbled under her gaze and backed off. "Uh, I don't know. Do you?"

Patricia laughed. "Oh, yes, definitely." She put her sunglasses back on. "Shall we go?"

"Could I put some clothes on, first?" I inquired.

"Long pants might be a good idea, but the rest is really up to you, dear," Patricia said, eying my upper torso again.

"I'll be right back," I said. "Don't get mauled by the cat."

"She'd never do such a thing," Patricia said as I went inside. She was talking to the cat, not me.

I didn't get any keys thrown at me when I came back out, so I pocketed my own and started towards my truck. Patricia's voice caught me up short.

"Where are you going? This way!" She sang, stepping off the porch, and heading towards her house. I realized she wasn't carrying a purse, or a tote, or anything, and narrowed my eyes.

Increasingly curious, I followed her in tentative silence. We reached her backyard garden and turned not right, towards her house, but left, towards the woods. Once we stepped into the dense trees there was a sort of path that only made itself apparent once we were on it. It serpentined through the trees and underbrush like a game trail even the game had abandoned. Patricia walked briskly, occasionally pulling down the remnants of a morning spider web, or pushing aside a branch.

The woods were fern-coated and surprisingly bright. I kept turning around to study the view of where we'd come from—looking out instead of looking in. The trees were sparser than I'd imagined, but the area still seemed overgrown. Ahead of us, at a slight angle, a fallen poplar trunk blocked our path. It seemed to disappear in both directions. Patricia put a hand to it and ducked underneath, knocking a little of the lifeless bark off as she went. I followed suit more awkwardly, disadvantaged by my height.

When it seemed as if we'd walked the length of a football field I asked, "Are we still on your property?"

"Oh, yes," she said, "Lot's a little triangular but it's five acres."

"Wow," I said. I didn't know Elmcroft had five-acre lots. Then I stepped around a little sapling in a bend of the trail and froze.

"Here we are dear," she said, picking her away towards our ultimate destination. It was the gawky skeleton of an abandoned greenhouse. A story-high circle of wrought-iron frames sprouted into a domed ceiling that seemed borne from ivy. The tendriled vines spiraled down the broader poles and pooled below before blending out into the underbrush around us. A timber door had long rotted away, but a cleared path led to the opening where it used to be. Patricia stepped forward to it before pausing to look back at me.

"Are you coming?" she asked.

I hadn't moved. I gaped at the structure. Time and the elements had punched out a third of its delicate glass panes. Those that remained were murky with seasonal grime. The iron framework of octagonal wall panels rose into ornate patterns of stylized fleur-de-lis. I started peering around the perimeter, searching for a crumbling retaining wall or some indication that we had just stepped into the English countryside. Surely these were the remnants of a Victorian conservatory, attached to a large and stately manor house. There was no European manor. I was looking at the relic of a free-standing solarium right in the middle of the jungle they call Appalachia. And it was breathtaking.

"How..." I started and trailed off, not completely sure of the order or nature of my questions.

"Yes well I'll explain dear, but do keep it quiet, the government doesn't exactly know it's here and God knows they'd find a way to tax it or condemn it, you know," she sniffed. She'd stepped back to my side now, realizing I needed a moment to absorb. "It's too treed in for aerial photography and just enough out of sight of my house, even in winter, that the land assessors have never even found it. How 'bout that!" She smiled proudly.

"But, so—what are those?" I pointed to unnatural smears of color peeking out from behind the ivy on some of the lower panes of glass.

"Oh," Patricia said with disgust "Paintball. The state may not have found it, but some kids did, years and years ago, thought it'd be a good place to stage a war."

"Ah. Too bad."

"Quite," Patricia agreed. "Rex owned this land, you know, before there was ever any subdivision. Before there was even a road. We lived in town during the heyday of Murgatroyd Garden Supply, so Rex could be close to the business, but he rented the house here to a sweet old widow who found the greenhouse when she was out walking her dog one day. It wasn't in quite such bad shape back then, and the woman had been a florist before she got married. She fixed it up a bit and rigged up all kinds of solar-powered heat and irrigation and used it to grow the most beautiful orchids, and then gave some to Rex every month as part of her rent. He sold them down at the Garden Supply. My goodness were they popular. Rex never did tell a single customer where they came from." She smiled.

"Who would have believed him?" I wondered. Evidence of functionality was scattered about the underbrush—shards of heavy ceramic, pieces of soft tubing, and crumbling cinder blocks painted black on the outside. It seemed like the greenhouse had expelled its insides into the forest, but I suspected roaming teenagers had helped.

"I don't think we ever did figure out who built it, or why," she continued. "We didn't even know it existed until the tenant found it. It was already old then. And no remains of any other buildings around here."

"Maybe there was a garden, though," I pondered, "or it could have been used to overwinter plants, or I guess maybe as a meditative solarium. Intended to be a little remote."

"Perhaps," Patricia said, hands on hips, looking up at it. "You know what I really think?"

"Pray tell," I said, eying her.

"Butterflies. I think it was a butterfly house. Wouldn't that be lovely, out here in the woods, raising butterflies?"

"Seems like they wouldn't need a house, out here in the woods," I said, but she frowned at me. "Or maybe they would," I allowed. "It'd have made a lovely butterfly house."

"You know, when Rex died," Patricia started, gulping forest air before she continued, "When he died, I really...well, I wanted to die too." Her lips pursed. On that drunken anniversary night she'd told me all about their relationship, but not this. It didn't sound like an exaggeration.

"I didn't do all that traveling because I wanted to; it was a necessary escape, a necessary distraction from myself. Didn't dare give myself time to think, in those days. When I was done traveling—when I couldn't take another step—it happened in Venice, you know, one night, riding a gondola under the bridges of back canals, looking up at all the lights and life above me. It happened that night, and I knew, and I booked my return flight for the next day and came back home, to the house here, to die.

"I had just put my bags down, in a kind of trance, and I was standing in my foyer, staring at the wall. The walls where for ten years I'd hung no pictures, painted no colors, invited no company. And the doorbell rang. And I opened it, and it was Leroy McGuff, standing there in grimy, coal-dust-covered overalls. And he was holding a bouquet of pristine white roses out to me and talking about being my new neighbor and how his wife thought roses were the perfect gift for every occasion and how he'd just stopped by to introduce himself. And he looked happy.

"And I couldn't process kindness, couldn't process happiness, then. I did not want a friend and I did not want help and I did not even want to be noticed. So I slammed the door in his face. And then I ran. I ran to the back of my house, and out the back door, and out into the woods, crashing along, not caring if I slammed into a tree or not; I wanted to slam into something. I was scarcely looking where I was going; I tripped on a branch, after a bit, and fell on my hands and knees. And I looked up—and this is what I saw," she smiled sadly and gestured to the greenhouse.

"Of course I knew it was back here, somewhere, the orchid woman had told us, but I'd never tried to find it for myself—I mean I was never at home anyway, and I'd kind of forgotten about it, or let it drift into myth or something. And do you know, Johnny, I went inside, and sat down—there are old benches inside, I'll show you in a moment—and I sat and looked at this magnificent beat-up old beauty, and realized I didn't want to die. I'm a beat-up old beauty too, you know."

She smiled brighter now, but then her face took another turn.

"And since that day—that day *years* ago—I haven't spoken a word to Leroy McGuff. I guess it was embarrassment, or guilt, or pride, or some sickly combination I had yet to resolve. I didn't heal instantly, you know. I was going to talk to Leroy one day; I was going to thank him, and apologize. I was going to tell him he saved my life. I was going to tell him he was too happy for me to bear, but that I was healthier now; that now I could be happy for him and with him. But it's too late now."

I watched a single, sober tear slide down Patricia's cheek. As it ran its course it stole some eye makeup. She wiped at it, smearing black across her face as she looked up at me.

"Took to you right off, of course," she patted a palm to my arm, "I've never seen you happy once."

"I used to be," I said.

"I know, dear."

SEVENTEEN

"Well, come on in," Pat said, tugging my arm. I obediently followed her forward, stepping onto the moss and leaf litter carpet of the interior. There were benches, or more likely repurposed shelves, running in a semicircle opposite the door. Most were covered in moss and ivy, but farthest from us, in the middle, a section had been cleared off for sitting. On each end sat an orchid plant; live, viable, bright orchids. The pair shot up from plastic containers that seemed impossibly small to support the elongated stems and showy flowers.

"Oh, well, now, I can't keep them here through the year or anything, place doesn't hold heat anymore with all this missing glass," Patricia said, noticing me eying the plants. "They usually live on my kitchen sills, you know. But they do just fine here through the summer, and I come out here all the time when the weather's nice. I think it rejuvenates them, being out here. Look at these, Johnny, have you ever seen anything so pretty?" She floated fingers between darkly variegated leaves and subtle pink brush marks on white lady slipper blooms.

"I bet this place was amazing when your tenant had it full of them," I said, looking around with new appreciation.

"I do wish I'd seen it then," Patricia agreed. She sat on the cleared bench between the flowers, motioning me to join her.

"Do you hear that?" I asked, ignoring her invitation. I stood in the middle of the floor with my head cocked to the side.

Out in the woods, opposite the direction of Patricia's house, distant synthesized noises and amplified voices echoed over the treetops. The sounds were distorted and strange, reaching us in bits and incomprehensible pieces. At first it was easy to think it was just the wind playing tricks with loose branches, or the shallow rapids of a nearby creek. But the patterns weren't natural or organic. Occasionally they were distinctly human. I raised an eyebrow at Patricia.

"I've never heard anything like that out here, Johnny. Doesn't sound like it's on my property but this land butts up against a pretty rural area up there." She was standing now, gazing in the direction of the mountain noises. "Kind of sounds like another game of beer pong. Don't you think, dear?"

"Not before noon on a Wednesday, I don't. Plus, it sounds like a loudspeaker. But I guess an amp and some bad music would do it."

"Well, I'd say it's some kind of public event, but kind of doubtful anything's going on back in those woods," Patricia pondered.

"Maybe it is, actually," I said, finally sitting on the bench. "Maybe it's a revival meeting."

"Oh, now, you could be onto something there," Pat mused, taking the seat beside me. We both leaned back in the peaceful solarium, listening to the faint commotion.

"Do you think the evangelicals are spilling our way?" I asked after a moment.

"I don't think so, Johnny. They're not getting any louder."

"Maybe God's keeping them at bay," I conjectured, glancing up past mullioned windows to the domed glass ceiling.

Patricia chuckled. "Yes dear," she said. "Or maybe it is just a game of beer pong. There's not much difference in the two, is there?"

I gave her half a grin, closing my eyes in the warmth of the approaching noon. More surprising than this property's dilapidated antique architecture was the capacity for peacefulness in its owner. It had never occurred to me that Patricia could be a calm person, or would isolate herself for contentment's sake. Was this where her strength came from? It wasn't just from the people she surrounded herself with? Had I peeked into her salvation? Or was I confusing it with my own? Sitting there within the framework of what was, I had a sense of painful hope; but it was fleeting, and I lost the answer as soon as I glimpsed it..

"I'm hungry," I finally said.

"Do you ever think we were made for greater things, honey?" Pat asked, surfacing from her own thoughts.

"Not really," I said. I didn't understand what she meant.

"Me neither," she laughed. "And if we were, we'd be too fucked up to know it. Well, lunchtime, Johnny! I need a drink."

I got up and stepped out of the greenhouse, giving a reverential nod to the structure that oozed with a zeitgeist at total odds with coal country. Patricia followed me out to the trail. I began picking my way along until her cell phone rang shrilly from her back pocket, making us both jump.

"Hello?" She answered.

I walked on ahead a few steps until I realized she wasn't following. I stepped away further to give her some privacy, and leaned my back against a tree. I could see her frowning down the trail.

"I see," she was saying. Her eyes were boring a hole into a nearby sycamore. The friction of her gaze might have been enough to set the tree on fire. She murmured acquiescent phrases, hung up, and then she exploded.

"How *dare* he," she started in a dangerously low tone. She power-walked past me before I could blink. "How dare he. HOW DARE HE!" she was screaming ahead of me now. I jogged a few steps to catch up and strode through her string of expletives until we emerged into her backyard. She motored on through the garden and up the steps of her porch, letting the screen door slam behind her as she disappeared into the house.

When I caught up to her in the kitchen she was already sitting on a bar stool, scotch glass in hand.

"I don't think it's a good idea to be a reactionary drinker," I suggested.

"I intended to come back and pour a drink long before that despicable excuse for a man called," she reported. I took a seat next to her.

"Giles?" I asked.

"Of course Giles," she said sharply.

"Do you want to talk about it?"

"Of course I don't want to talk about it. I don't need to talk about it. If he wants to cancel our date, leave me high and dry, abandon me and treat me as a lowlife suspect, why should I care about that. Why should I care?" she asked again, eyes entreating me. "I mean, my shovel is missing. I understand that. I went to bed early, alone, I don't have an alibi. People might have mentioned I wasn't on the best terms with Leroy. Giles might have a superior reminding him about fraternization with persons of interest. I understand that. I understand all of that," she took a big gulp of her drink. "But how could he!"

I thought she was going to cry, so I spoke quickly. "You just said it: it's not his choice. Breaking off with you isn't an indication he thinks you're guilty. It's just his job description."

"No one takes their job that seriously," she said. Her right ring fingernail was scratching at an etching of the Pantheon on her glass.

"He's a serious man. He does not think you killed anyone. He's just doing things by the books."

"Rex never did things by the books," Patricia sniffed.

"Lotta fish in the sea," I said. I got up to find the food I could smell. I opened her fridge and stood in front of it, frowning.

"It's in the crock pot, dear," she advised me. "Make yourself a bowl."

I obeyed and ladled something like a seafood boil into a bowl. It was an array of jumbo shrimp, red potatoes, sausage rounds, onion slices, and quartered corn cobs. I dribbled some of the spicy smelling broth over all of it and put the bowl in front of Patricia. Then I turned back to fill one for myself.

"Thank you, dear," she said, looking unenthusiastically at the food. I was nearly salivating.

"How long have you been up?" I asked wonderingly, punching a fork into a perfectly cooked potato.

"Six, dear. I always get up at six."

"That's...ambitious."

"Thank you, dear," she intoned again, scarcely

listening.

"Do you want to be alone?" I asked.

"Oh hell no Johnny, I'm sorry," she blinked hard and started moving food around her bowl. I'll be fine. Please do stay."

"What do you want to talk about," I asked, not knowing what to say.

"It used to be men just ate my food and didn't concern themselves with my priorities." Her tone was one of genuine wistfulness.

"I would actively like to hear about what you're prioritizing, Patricia," I returned, the first taste of food imbuing me with a sense of indefinite patience.

"I'm unfortunately still prioritizing that abhorrent excuse for a detective and my misplaced feelings for him," she spat, "so perhaps you should pick the topic.

"What did you two even talk about together, anyway?" I asked through a mouthful of potato. "Doesn't seem like you have that much in common…"

Patricia gave me a smug grin. "Oh, you know, the philosophical ramifications of vigilante killing, politics in a red state, American Crow terminology. Whatever, anything, we talked about it all! We were very sympatico, you know." She stabbed a fork into a piece of sausage but didn't put it in her mouth.

"Oh," I said. "So…say, what is your alibi?" I looked up finally from my lunch.

"My what!" she leered sideways at me.

"I mean, Monday night. What were you doing before you came home and saw Zeb Fix? And you really just went to bed that early? What do you mean the police don't have an alibi for you?"

"I can't tell you," she said.

"Can't tell me, or can't tell the police?" I eyed her.

She looked at me sideways over her scotch glass. "It's nothing really, Johnny. I meet acquaintances sometimes on weekday evenings to perform certain...services for them. Monday evening though...well, he's a public official, you see, and I wouldn't want the police harassing him." She poured herself more scotch.

I tried to recover my lower jaw and squinted at Patricia. She was an attractive woman, in a vivacious, well-aged sort of way.

"What sort of, uh..." I cleared my throat "...services?"

Patricia's eyes widened. "Why, I never!" She seemed to be casting about for something to throw at me. "I am not a prostitute, Johnny Jepko!"

"Well, sure, of course not," I leaned back, away from her. "I just...well I mean it's none of my business, really—"

"I do Tarot readings, you ingrate," she fumed, "and on Monday I was reading for a city councilman. Honestly, Jepko, get your mind out of the gutter!"

"Tarot readings?" I mused. "Like with the death cards and whatnot? Like a psychic? I mean, that's a legitimate form of entertainment, isn't it? I don't think you, or a city councilman, would get in trouble for that."

"He's also a Baptist minister," she grumbled into her glass.

"Oh. Ah. Yeah, okay. A little Leviticus entanglement, eh?"

"It's not funny, John. Discretion is my biggest selling point. And it's my most lucrative hobby."

"How many other side businesses you have going on, Pat?" I wondered as I took my last bite. I went for seconds, not expecting an answer.

"Don't you dare!" She was beside me in an instant, rapping my arm with a wooden ladle before I reached the crock pot. "You're going to ruin your dinner," she added.

"What's for dinner?" I asked, rubbing my arm.

"Leftovers," she gestured to the crock pot.

"You necromancers are all the same," I said.

EIGHTEEN

"You want to go to the botanical gardens this afternoon?" Julia's clear voice asked over the phone.

"The what?" I said sleepily, holding the cell away from my face so I could see the time. It was seven o'clock Friday morning. I suppose I had been the one to tell her I didn't believe in texting.

"The botanical gardens, John. The ones Patricia helped found, volunteers at...you know?"

"I did not know," I countered. I gave a little jolt as I half rolled in my bed and came face to face with the mangy calico. She licked her lips.

"I'll pick you up at three, I just want to go for a bit, have a fluff piece to do on site there next week. Okay?"

"Sure," I said. I was too tired to think of an excuse.

"Break's over gotta get back to it, see you then!" She clicked silent.

I sat up.

"Fuck," I said to the cat.

*   *   *

That afternoon Julia pulled up in her shiny little Jetta. I was thinking about how to sneak a couple of Corinthian columns into a banal townhouse design without the homeowners noticing. I gave the blueprint one more second of empty staring and shut the laptop.

As she stepped out of the car Julia beamed. "Oh, what a nice day! Perfect for a little garden walk. And how are you?" She stepped forward to kiss me on the cheek. She might have kissed me on the lips, but I pretended I didn't see her coming and turned my head.

"Fine," I said, trying not to look at her. "How was your week?" I hadn't seen her since Sunday's excruciating brunch. Julia Winfield was accomplished and intoxicating, and I had no idea why she'd set her sights on me so quickly. After I had realized that first one-night-stand was anything but, I'd felt tricked. My eyes gravitated to her sundress and my brain warily took her all in.

"Oh great, great, trying lots of new stuff at the station. Loving the field time they're giving me. Had an interesting chat with Pat's beau the other day, too, off the record," she winked. "Ready to go?"

"Want me to drive?" I asked.

"Oh no, no, allow me, I left the AC running," she smiled broadly. "Plus, this was my idea, wasn't it!"

I had already removed my keys from my pocket, and now I leaned in to surrender them to the table. "All ready then," I said.

I folded myself into her Jetta and we were off to see plants. As we pulled out of my drive I looked wistfully in the direction of Patricia's hidden greenhouse. I wondered if she'd ever told Julia about it. I doubted it.

I started a little as I caught myself scanning Leroy McGuff's yard. Instead of seeing the waving man himself, my eyes ran into crime scene leftovers. Julia had slowed at the bottom of the drive, and she was looking, too.

"Monday night, huh. Are you okay? I heard you...found him," she said carefully.

"It wasn't my best Monday," I said, not meeting her eyes. She continued down the road, realizing I wasn't going to be chatty about it.

"Well," she said instead, "I hear the crape myrtle are blooming!"

I stared at her from the passenger seat, a little amazed at her self-control. We rode on in silence. Julia was the perfect package, smart and beautiful. What was she doing with me? Darby had matched my darkness. Julia always seemed to be reflecting light that wasn't there.

The Charleston Botanical Garden was down one of those infamous West Virginia back roads where GPS failed, and so did the pavement.

"Almost there," Julia said as the road turned to gravel. We jerked across some potholes to a handmade wooden sign announcing our destination. The road opened up surprisingly into a huge, flat parking area. Julia pulled in beside several other vehicles next to an unremarkable wooden lodge.

"I'm gonna go grab us a map," she said, "hang tight!"

She hadn't really given me time to do anything else. I finally made out the "Visitor's Center" sign scrawled over the building's door. Julia popped back out in no time. She was a classic blonde vision bouncing down the porch steps. I groaned inwardly.

Two screaming children burst past her as she re-donned her sunglasses, and she pulled up short. She waited for them to pass and strode over to me, taking my arm.

"Aren't they sweet!" she observed.

Two fair-haired boys had ended their mad dash with a tumble into the grass off the parking area. After a brief bout of shirt-yanks and dizzy circling, they collapsed on their backs and rolled about with high pitched laughter. They stilled after a few seconds, pointing to cumulus clouds and blinding themselves with sunlight. A distant parent yelled through the brush and they scampered away, disappearing along a path.

"Charming," I said.

She frowned at me.

"Well, this way to the dogwood berries," she said, map in hand. She motioned towards the path the young boys had taken. We stepped forward into the gardens, passing by tiny plaques announcing scientific names of the flora.

"An outdoor museum," I noted.

"Would you just look at those hydrangea," Julia said, pointing into a myriad of colorful blooming bushes to our left.

"So you talked to Detective Giles?" I asked as we weaved down the path.

"Ah yes. It was off record, of course, nothing official," she laughed lightly. "But you'll never believe. It turns out Pat's shovel isn't the only one missing from the neighborhood."

"Really?" I turned to her now, my interest piqued.

"Really. So is Dillon Meers'."

I stopped full now, staring at her. "How do they know that?" I asked.

"Well when they first investigated the crime scene unit happened to photograph it. It was sitting clear as day on his side deck," she continued, pulling me forward. "And I suppose some police officer went to check, after McGuff was killed, and sure enough, it's not there anymore. Oh!"

"What?" I asked.

"That magnolia," she pointed again. "Look at those blooms!"

I tried to drown my frustration in a hard swallow.

"Detective Giles didn't say so, but he implied that the number-one suspect is the missing Dillon Meers," she said, winking at me. "I think the theory is: he came back to his house Monday to do who knows what, and poor Leroy saw him from across the street. Being a wanted man, Meers couldn't have a witness to his visit. He grabbed the first weapon he saw, and headed across the road. Apparently Mr. McGuff was quite a friendly guy, and wouldn't have suspected a thing. Meers must have walked right up, starting to explain his absence or something, and bam."

She stopped to read the plaque underneath a large sumac tree. Then she unfolded the map and studied it again.

"Bam?" I asked, "Bam! A wanted and dangerous man approached him carrying a shovel and Leroy McGuff just stood there?"

"Well," she stood back up straight, "*someone* approached him with a shovel and he just stood there, after all. And as far as I understand it, for years before Dillon Meers was a wanted, dangerous man, he was probably just—"

"A friendly neighbor," I finished for her.

"Yes. A friendly neighbor."

I pretended to mull that over. I didn't buy it for a second.

"What did Patricia have to say?" I asked.

"Oh, I haven't told her," Julia said quickly. "We can't report it, so technically I shouldn't have told you, but…" She winked at me again. I was thoroughly rankled. I told myself my ire was borne of loyalty to Patricia, but I wasn't fooling myself.

"So, having known me all of two weeks you're better friends with me than Patricia now," I said in undisguised accusation..

"Well, we are seeing each other…"

"You mean we're fucking," I interrupted.

She looked up from the map, nonplussed. I watched her big beautiful eyes narrow just a little.

"I'm sorry," she said with the slightest edge. "I suppose we haven't had that conversation yet. But you've obviously reached some conclusions on your own." She looked at me, gaze unwavering. Her eyes had a hint of worry, but were otherwise bright and patient. She was waiting for me to say something. She wasn't going to get angry, and it was pissing me off.

"Where are we going," I said, pointing to the map.

She opened the map again and started walking, slowly. I followed.

Nervous tension propelled us along the various paths, until the one we were on stopped at the foot of a grassy hill. It was clear of trees and open to the sky.

"I want to see the view," Julia said without pausing, and we walked up the slope to a meadow-topped plateau. A centrally placed arched trellis stood, its wooden slats smothered in fading, flaking white paint. Recently bloomed clematis vines clung to the sides, but the flowers were all dead or dying. Julia touched one of the few remaining purple petals and rested her hand on the archway. The view was amazing. Our slight elevation put us high enough above tree level to see almost 360 degrees of blue mountains.

"Why did you come here with me today, Johnny?" Julia asked, looking at the mountains, and not me

"I don't know," I said, which I thought was nicer than saying *insomnia-fueled momentum.*

"It's just that I get the distinct impression you don't

want to be here. That you don't want to be with me. So I'm trying to understand why you are."

"It was a mistake," I said. "I mean...I mean I guess we should stop seeing each other."

"Have I done something to offend you?" She asked, turning to me now.

"No. Not at all. I just..." I trailed off.

"People get married here, you know. They rent the whole place out."

I blinked.

"I mention it because you just dumped me under the wedding arch."

"Oh...oh," I looked up at the trellis guiltily. "I didn't know."

"Well, let's go," Julia said. She folded up the map and stuffed it in her purse. I doubted that she'd really needed it in the first place. There were only so many ways to go. As we strode back down the hill into the gardens I looked at her sideways. Her lips were a little tighter than normal, but she walked steadily with her eyes forward. Here was someone who was waiting to explode on her own terms. Here was someone with full emotional control. Suddenly she was out of my league and not of my world. I guessed the latter had always been the problem.

After a silent car ride she dropped me off at my house.

"Goodbye, Johnny Jepko," she said.

"Goodbye," I said, heading to my deck.

She leaned out of the driver's side window. "What is *wrong* with you?"

I turned and looked at her but said nothing.

She pulled away.

*   *   *

To make myself feel better I went grocery shopping. I had been the one to do the hurting, of course, but pain tends to backfire.

There were few places I liked more than the produce aisle of a grocery store. I found the rows of fruits and vegetables breathtaking: here was one entire human need, quantified in endless variety, and ripe for the picking, yet no picking was required. This was technology I could appreciate.

I filled my basket with a couple types of citrus and a several grillable vegetables I knew Patricia didn't grow in her garden. I was starting to feel better. I stepped into the checkout line.

The woman in front of me looked to be in her seventies, and well put together. She wore a flowing teal shawl and her short silver hair was tastefully styled over diamond stud earrings. I happened to look at her cart and did a double take. It was full to the brim with only two things: gallon upon gallon of iced tea, and bag after bag of Milano chocolate cookies. At first I thought she must be shopping for a book club or church event. But there was no differentiation in tea or cookie; they were all identical to their brethren. No group of people could be satisfied with such a blatant lack of options. But one very habit-prone person could.

The woman noticed my slack-jawed staring. She finished writing her check in a flurry and grabbed her cart to go. I had forgotten people still used checks; I stared at that, too. As I set my basket in front of the cashier, the woman turned back to me with a glare.

"What is *wrong* with you," she spat.

I looked up to the young cashier to see if she was going to chime in, maybe complete the hat trick. She looked embarrassed and started punching in vegetable codes. She didn't ask if I wanted paper or plastic. I watched her lips twitch in a suppressed grin.

Status quo restored, I left the store.

NINETEEN

"Did you know I was born exactly 100 years after Darwin died?" Darby asked me once from the other side of a chess set. The plastic pieces sat on rolled-out vinyl board on my coffee table. Back then my furniture wasn't buried under a metric ton of paper stacks. Darby had purchased the chess set for my apartment, which she liked to remind me was lacking in "games and plants and fun stuff."

"I did not," I said, pushing a black pawn towards her. She'd insisted on using the white pieces. I later realized she did that so she could pull a green sharpie from her purse and draw intricate little faces on them. At any given moment not all of her active pieces were actually on the board. They took turns transforming into her green-faced effigies. It made it kind of hard to play.

I smiled at her.

"Does that mean you're *particularly* genetically programmed to succeed?" I asked. She put the finishing touches on her rook and returned it to the board to take out my pawn.

She looked up at me with eyes drowning in need. She was about as predictable as a dice roll on the moon.

"What's the matter?" I asked, cocking my head to the side.

She sat up and crawled across the chessboard to me, sending queens and kings skittering off the coffee table to the carpet.

"Kiss me," she said when her face was inches from mine, and in those words was all the sad desperation that I was always too happy to hear.

*   *   *

It was with no small amount of trepidation that I accepted a Saturday night invitation to attend something at Patricia's. From my kitchen window I could see at least one extra car in her driveway and hear the extra unction in her voice. It was a trap, to be sure. But none of the cars were Julia's, so I leaned back from the sill and said okay. Sometimes it was best to take Pat's ambushes head-on. I wasn't feeling social, but considering that I never felt social, I could scarcely use that as an excuse.

I hadn't even finished rapping on the back door when it flew open. To my surprise, the woman swaying in front of me was a shit-faced Kim Controy. Her usually neat bun was disassembled into so many wisps it looked like her whole head might fly away. I didn't take too long blinking because she didn't allow me that sort of time. She pulled me inside by the arm and at a volume unbecoming of a librarian announced: "Ladies! The beefcake is here!" which is when I first thought I might be in trouble.

Kim led me a few steps inside and flitted away. To my left, Patricia and Sherry had heads bowed over a laptop on the living room couch, pointing and typing and murmuring. The number of wine glasses scattered around the room suggested a dozen more guests might be lurking down the hall. If so, they were silent. The two women appeared to be the only other people in the house.

Kim had disappeared into the kitchen and now tripped back in her long skirt, which clearly wasn't used to such speed. Her plain black heels were abandoned at the living room entrance, and she slid over the kitchen tile in stocking feet.

"Easy there," I said, stepping forward to maneuver her slight frame to a stop before she catapulted into the island.

"Oh thank you, thank you," she looked abashed for maybe one second before meeting my gaze and exploding into raucous laughter. "Here," she offered me an over-filled wine glass, taking a sip from her own through wine-stained lips.

"I never drink red," she laughed, and then sobering, "just such a hard day today. Such a hard day."

I nodded, wondering what kinds of hardships librarians encountered besides maybe the threat of extinction.

"Well, no matter! Not an easy week for you either, I know. Come on," she grabbed my arm again and escorted me to the living room. I didn't know if she was referring to my finding a dead body, or self-destructing with Julia, or both.

"Okay, okay now here," Patricia was saying to Sherry and pointing to the screen. Sherry's hands were poised above the keyboard, like an attentive student ready to take notes.

"Dislikes," Patricia began as Sherry typed, "Practical jokes, surprise parties, comedy, karaoke, hugs, displays of joy, beautiful women, breathing." She had slowly lifted her eyes as she spoke until she was staring directly at me. That's when

I knew for sure I was in trouble.

"What are you doing?" I asked.

Kim Controy suddenly blinded me with a cell phone camera flash from the left. She giggled.

"Making you an online dating profile, dear," Pat said through a plastered-on smile.

Nobody ambushed like Patricia Murgatroyd.

"You're what?" I asked, and not because I hadn't heard her.

I circled around the couch to see the laptop screen, which sure enough featured a user-friendly questionnaire for the lonely.

Sherry, who had either sensed my tone or read Pat's last few words, turned suddenly, looking concerned. "Pat told us you had a breakup, honey. We got to talking, and well, we thought this might be a fun distraction! It's a silly idea, I guess. I'm afraid there was some wine involved." She eyed Patricia and Kim, and I recalled her mentioning before that she didn't drink.

"Surprise!" Pat said. She was still smiling, but in the way people do when they'd rather be throttling you. Sherry's innocence was believable, and Kim appeared too inebriated to influence herself, much less anyone else. I had no doubt who had inserted this particular plan into the night's activities.

"Oh, Kim, hon, you might want to put that down," Sherry said in a rush. Kim was across the room handling a glass figurine so daintily it seemed certain she would drop it.

"It's a bluebird of happiness," Kim said, and her voice choked into a half-sob.

"Oh dear," Sherry said, setting the laptop aside and rising from the couch. She whisked a few Kleenex from a box on the end table and was at Kim's side in an instant, trading the bird for a tissue in one fluid motion. She returned the blue glass to the shelf and put one arm around Kim's shoulders, the other deftly moving the wine glass out of reach.

"Come here, now, let's sit down." Sherry shooed Patricia from the couch. Patricia finally dropped her glare and allowed herself to be herded out of the way. She got up, and collapsed regally into an armchair. I sat down in the one farthest from her.

"Are you sure you want me here? I don't want to interrupt your fun," I said, looking from the laptop to Pat.

She took a big gulp of wine. "How could you," she said.

I could tell she'd probably had as much to drink as Kim Controy, but her eyes were clear and angry and her speech even. There was nothing quite like the composure of a practiced alcoholic.

"What did she say?" I asked, swallowing. Kim sobbed quietly on the couch.

"What, so you can deny it? She didn't say anything. She's classier than that. I could barely squeeze out of her that it happened at all," she fumed. "How could you!"

"Well I didn't exactly plan to let it get—"

"And under a wedding arch!"

"That was unintentional. I—"

"It was despicable," she clarified.

"Look, am I not allowed to break up with someone? People break up every day. These things happen. I—" This time I was interrupted by a phlegm-laced gasp for breath. "Is she okay?" I looked over to the pair on the couch.

"Don't change the subject," Pat snapped.

"Patricia," Sherry spoke up sternly, "Your tone is upsetting her."

"The widow McGuff upset her, not me," Pat said harshly, and Kim Controy started wailing anew.

"Christ," I said, staring at this new, vindictive Patricia.

"Kim spent a few hours with Jolene McGuff this afternoon, helped her around the house with some things, and funeral arrangements, you know," Sherry said, half explaining to me, half distracting the room from Patricia. "Jolene does her hair, you know. They've gotten pretty close over the years. It was a rough afternoon on both of them, I think."

"Ah," I said, understanding. I hadn't seen Jolene since that night, crumpled in my arms in the grass. But I could imagine the reality of the situation hitting home a few days later, the numbness lifting, just a little, to let in the soul-crushing logistics of death. If Kim Controy had been her rock when that storm hit, it looked like Kim was crumbling now. And why not, I thought. Everyone needs a break.

"Should I make coffee?" I asked Sherry.

"Maybe just some water for her, honey, thanks," she said, smoothing out Kim's hair.

I retreated to the kitchen for the water and had a sudden epiphany about Patricia.

"Giles didn't dump you, you know," I said to her as I came back into the living room, stopping to hand a glass of water to Sherry.

"What?" Patricia asked, startled.

"He hasn't dumped you. He's just putting things on hold. Giles isn't doing to you what I did to Julia," I tried to explain.

"Well of course not," Pat said, but the rage in her face had lessened. I could see a soft grin on Sherry's mouth from the corner of my eye.

"You know there's another missing shovel," I continued. "Dillon Meers' shovel. It was on his deck when they scoped out the house weeks ago and it's gone now."

"What!" Pat said again, this time putting her drink down and sitting up a little straighter.

"Yeah. So they have a real suspect now, I guess."

Sherry visibly shivered. "I just hate to think about that man still hanging around here somewhere," she said quietly. I had the feeling she wasn't a person who used the word "hate" a lot.

Kim had stopped crying and looked to be on a despondent path to sobriety. I had already planned to pretend that I hadn't seen her tonight. I figured she'd want it that way.

The high trill of a cell phone echoed from the kitchen.

"Grab me that thing, would you dear," Patricia said, motioning with her wine glass.

I got up again and retrieved the cell phone. I saw "Silas Giles" on the screen right before handing it over and decided it was a good time to go back to the kitchen and get myself a refill.

Patricia was still had the phone to her face when I came back. Sherry and Kim were giggling at something on the laptop, which I hoped was a viral cat video, and not anything to do with me.

"Oh goodness," Pat was saying. A weird mixture of delight and horror spread over her face. A few moments later she hung up and looked around the room. The three of us stared at her like dogs that had heard the treat bag open.

"I am no longer a person of interest!" she exclaimed.

"We all know you're not interesting," I said. "What else did he say?"

She shot me a look of reproach. "They found Dillon Meers' shovel," she said. "Down the road, thrown in a culvert. It doesn't have any fingerprints on it. But it has blood."

"Oh goodness," Sherry said.

"Leroy McGuff's blood," Pat finished.

Kim Controy burst out crying again.

"That's ridiculous," I contributed. "If there aren't fingerprints on it then anybody could still be a suspect."

"I guess the detective just really likes me." Patricia smirked before taking a long sip of wine. "Who wants to watch a movie!"

TWENTY

When I was ten I had a baseball card collection that rivaled oxygen as my reason for living. Everywhere I went I took my favorites with me in a little protective case I'd made by stapling the edges of two index cards together. To deter would-be thieves I'd taken a red marker, and in my best ten-year-old script I'd written: "JOHNNY'S PROPERTY," on the outside. I'd had to look up how to spell "property" in the big Oxford dictionary my parents kept in the living room. Before I even got to the P's I almost dropped the heavy tome twice. But the cards were worth it.

On car rides I used to pull them out and thumb through them slowly, spending time with each one, memorizing and studying. My father was trying to get a clear answer from me on a family trip once and I, mid-tantrum, was ignoring him to look through my cards.

He reached an arm behind the driver's seat and grabbed the handful from me. I didn't stop screaming when he cranked down the window, or when he chucked them out of it and they flew in all directions behind us down Interstate 64. I stopped screaming when I saw the shiny gold capitol dome, teary face pressed to the car window glass. After that I got into Legos. Dad probably couldn't tear down buildings.

*   *   *

I was wedged between a stack of Architectural Digest magazines and a long cardboard box at the center of my living room. I could see the staircase; I couldn't figure out how to get to the staircase. It was Sunday morning. I'd skipped the movie session the night before and gotten a decent night's sleep, arising early to get a head start on the work week. Progress had become a bit stagnant.

I shoved hard to my right, and the cardboard moved a little; it felt heavy, like something was in it. I contorted my arm down and pulled a flap up, then dug through several layers of packing material. It was the floor lamp I'd never unpacked. I realized it was a little dim in here, with two of three bulbs out in the relatively inaccessible overhead light. Or maybe I could access it, if I moved some stacks and stood on the edge of the coffee table. That didn't sound safe, so I rifled through to the lamp stand and pulled it halfway out of the box. That might remind me to set it up later.

I glanced back at the staircase, half a room away. I removed my glasses and polished them idly on my shirt, then replaced them, hoping to see a solution. There had been a path as recently as last week, I was sure, although I hadn't been up there in awhile. The house was plenty big for one person, and I'd have been fine just using the first floor. But I'd managed to fill it with all the paper I didn't throw away.

Sighing, I squeezed forward and took a giant step up onto more cardboard. It held my weight but tilted a little, throwing me into a pile of newspapers that went sliding off to the left. I pushed off anyway and hurtled myself forward, eventually stumbling down into the clear space at the bottom of the steps.

I dusted myself off and scaled the stairs, whistling a little as I turned into a guest bedroom, sans bed. The closet door was ajar, and I opened it curiously. I was greeted by an angry cat hiss. I considered shutting her in there, but didn't relish the eventual clean up.

I redirected towards the two small filing cabinets on the other side of the otherwise empty room. I unlocked one and began leafing through labeled tabs. I pulled out the files I needed and cast about for my stapler. It used to live on top of the filing cabinet, but that was back in the apartment. I turned a slow 180, pondering. The only place it could be, unfortunately, was one of the unpacked boxes buried in the living room. I sighed again and made my way back downstairs, the cat following on my heels. When we got to the last step, she jumped underneath the rail into the stacks and disappeared through a tunnel of some sort. She resurfaced at the edge of the kitchen, meowed plaintively.

Several minutes later I popped out, a few pages of notepaper sloshing along the floor in my wake. I leaned down and collected them, placing them on top of the nearest stack. I fed the cat and then slid the deck door open a little, poking my head out.

"Want coffee?" I asked Patricia. She was sitting in one of the coil-spring chairs, bobbing gently.

"Do you have Kahlua?" she asked, not turning around.

"Maybe," I lied. I ducked back in and made a pot of coffee, making no attempt to engage the liquor cabinet.

"How was movie night?" I asked a few minutes later, stepping out to the deck and handing her a hot mug.

"Oh just wonderful, just wonderful," she said.

"Do you have a stapler?" I asked.

"Well yes," she said. "Somewhere. Maybe in Rex's old office things. Who in the world still staples, Johnny, it's the age of faxing!"

I blinked. "You're several ages behind," I said.

She took a sip of the coffee and grimaced. "I'm classic, you mean. Well come on," she said, "let's go get it now."

Any animosity of the night before had disappeared, although I suspected her rush to leave my deck was really a rush to doctor her coffee. I followed her down off the deck and we entered her kitchen a minute later. As soon as I sat down on a bar stool, the front door bell rang.

"Did you hear a car?" Patricia asked, setting down a bottle of rum and heading for the door.

"Nope," I answered, taking a sip of coffee and looking at my watch. It wasn't even nine.

I had a line of sight down the entrance hallway to the front door, and got a glimpse as Patricia opened it. A man stood on the other side. I held my breath. He was holding a pristine bouquet of white roses. I remembered Pat talking about the last time a man arrived at her front door with white flowers, but that man was dead now.

It was the tall, graying Detective Giles playing the role of Leroy McGuff's ghost. I got off my seat quickly and stepped towards them, not sure how Patricia was going to react.

"Oh...oh my!" Patricia said, sounding pleased.

"I was checking out the crime scene," Giles motioned behind him, "thought I'd put these to use and invite you to brunch."

"Well I'd be delighted," Patricia said, taking the flowers with a smile.

Giles looked past her and noticed me lingering. I

couldn't tell if the look that passed over his face was surprise or consternation. Probably both.

"Good morning, Jepko," he said stoically.

"Morning," I replied, returning to my coffee and leaving it up to Patricia to ease the tension.

"Oh, Johnny's just borrowing a stapler, don't mind him," she said on cue, reaching above the island for a vase. The detective had wrapped a handkerchief around the thorny stems, and she peeled it carefully away before situating the roses. I sipped my coffee and waited to see if she was going to whip out the gold spray paint. She didn't. Giles took a seat caddy corner to me.

"Nowhere that opens for brunch before ten, dear," she spoke to the detective, "would you like some coffee?"

"Sure, thanks," Giles said, and then looked curiously as Patricia set up the plainly empty coffee pot.

"How long you been here?" He asked with bemusement, nodding to the empty pot.

"Oh, just got here, we were drinking my coffee," I said, "Er, from my house. Or deck, I mean—"

Patricia stepped in, rolling her eyes at me. "I sometimes watch the sunrise from Johnny's deck. You have to try it sometime, Silas. Best view in the neighborhood. And he doesn't mind, he's usually fast asleep anyway."

The detective looked skeptical and slightly confused, but shrugged. "I'll take your word for it."

"Would you and your lady like to join us?" Giles turned to me, "Julia?"

I cringed and sent a skirting glance in Patricia's direction.

"We're actually not seeing each other anymore," I said, ducking my head to sip more coffee.

"Oh, sorry to hear that. Well you're still welcome to join us," he said. I suppose he found himself trapped.

"That's okay, I actually have some work I need to get done this morning. Thanks though," I offered.

Patricia raised an eyebrow at me and handed Giles a cup of steaming coffee.

"Top off?" she asked me.

"Please," I said, holding my mug out for her pour.

"You're working early for a Sunday, aren't you Silas?" Patricia said as she sat down to join us. She'd added more coffee to her own mug, but no more rum, I noticed.

"There have been some developments. Needed to fill in Mrs. McGuff on some things," he said.

"Oh really? You mean the shovel?" Patricia asked with interest.

"Assuming you're not a sociopath—" he looked at Patricia.

"Only on Tuesdays," she assured him.

"—then the only logical explanation, or logical motive, for McGuff's...incident...is that Dillon Meers, as we've suspected, is still in the area. McGuff saw him trying to break back into his own house, and—"

"Oh yes, yes, Johnny and I had already thought of that," Patricia said quickly.

The detective eyed us both before continuing. "And killed him so he wouldn't report seeing him. Which pairs nicely with the fact that we've already charged him with a similar crime."

"What similar crime?" I asked.

"Killing his wife." McGuff said.

"Charged?" Patricia piped up.

"Those gloves with gunshot residue we found in the closet," the detective said. "Forensics came back. Had her blood on them. Pretty much made the case for the prosecutors. Besides which, it wouldn't be the first time Zebulon Fix had lied to the police. He kind of makes a habit of it. You haven't seen him around, have you?" He said, turning to me.

"Not since Monday," I answered, wishing I had some of Patricia's rum in my coffee.

Giles was certainly in a sharing mood this morning. I wondered if it was his way of making amends with Patricia.

"Not to mention," he went on, "the more we talked with her friends and coworkers, the more...dire her relationship with her husband seemed to be. As far as we could tell he wasn't physically abusive, but he was everything but. According to her friends she was even having doubts before the marriage. She ignored them, I guess."

"Easy to confuse the fluttering of stomach butterflies with the fluttering of red flags," quipped Patricia.

My stomach was fluttering, and it wasn't butterflies. I couldn't exactly speak up and insist that it *was* a suicide. That she'd left the note with me. That we were having an affair. That I had moved into the empty house next door to hers three months after I found her alone on her couch, dead. I couldn't really say any of those things. I didn't want to say any of those things. You could kill someone without pulling the trigger yourself, after all.

"I hope you get him," I said.

Giles looked up at me, sensing the voracity that had leaked out in my tone.

"We will, son," he said reassuringly.

He stood up with his coffee and wandered over to the window above Patricia's kitchen sink, scanning the view.

"Going to be a nice day," he said, looking out across the cul de sac. He could probably see the very corner of Leroy's yard from there. Jolene's yard now, I guessed.

"Where shall we brunch, Silas?" Pat asked, watching him.

"Timber Grill?" came the expected answer.

"Oh yes, that'll be just fine. Well we can hit the road pretty soon. Johnny, let me grab you that stapler, dear, if I can find it." She disappeared down a back hallway.

Giles was still at the window, looking a little puzzled, when Patricia returned and laid the black stapler in front of me. I blew the dust off of it.

"What I still don't understand," Pat said, looking thoughtful, "is where is *my* shovel?"

"Is that the Controy kid out on the road, getting chased by a squirrel?" Giles asked. He took a thoughtful sip of coffee.

TWENTY-ONE

A few days later at Leroy McGuff's funeral I watched Jason Controy squirming in his seat. He sat between overprotective parents, towering over both. The church pews were packed to the gills and the air was stifling. I could feel sweat dripping down my back as I watched the teenager wipe beads from his own forehead with a sleeve.

The pastor started another prayer I squinted upwards, not in search of God, but in hopes that the sun streaking through the high stained glass windows might put me out of my misery once and for all. I wasn't convinced that the air conditioning was even on. Regardless, this many people in a space this size on a July afternoon wouldn't have been anything but sweltering. I kicked a loafer at the floor and tried to ignore Patricia. She sat to my left and accompanied her sniffles with almost constant hand-wringing.

"Those who walk uprightly enter into peace," the pastor was saying in a low, booming voice. "They find rest as they lie in death."

Murmurs of "amen" cropped up around the group. It was as if everybody were trying to sing a single note, but no one came in on the beat. I opened and closed my mouth, feigning participation. Little hiccups of tears started up around me when the black-garbed Jolene McGuff stepped to the front. Her hand was vise-gripped around a tissue that she held pressed to her mouth before speaking.

Now I squirmed too. The tearful widow was a little too heartbreaking to watch. I felt sad and awkward and helpless. I cast about for something else to take my attention. I noticed Detective Giles over Patricia's shoulder. He was moving slowly around the perimeter of the chamber. Like me, he wasn't looking at the widow. I watched him watching the guests, eyes roving down the length of each pew. Besides half the coal miners in West Virginia, the entire population of Elmcroft subdivision seemed to be in attendance.

Patricia elbowed me and leaned towards my ear. I'd never seen her wearing black before, but she'd managed to top it off with an overabundance of blue eye shadow.

"You wanna little nip, dear?" she whispered. I rolled my eyes and shook my head. She gave our neighbors a few furtive glances and reached in her purse, producing a flask. I stared straight ahead. She shrugged and flipped the flask up against her lips in my periphery.

I felt eyes on the back of my head and glanced back to see Julia staring daggers at me. She was wearing a figure-hugging black cocktail dress with lines as severe as her expression. I rolled my eyes back off of her as fast as I could, hoping my grimace wasn't obvious.

Jolene McGuff was soon rendered speechless by tears, and a female relative escorted her back to a front-row seat. The closed coffin lay serenely at the front of the room. I pretended it was empty, or had some generic person in it rather than the abused body of my neighbor.

"They're doing the interment up on Kanawha Mountain for the family," Patricia stage-whispered across to me.

"So we don't have to go to that?" I asked.

"You're off the hook," she said, taking another swig from her flask.

The pastor wrapped up and people began to stir in their seats and rise. As the crowd filed out, I marveled at how popular a guy Leroy had been. Or maybe the manner of death was the attraction.

Sweltering in sun and guilt, I waited in the parking lot. Patricia bogarted the attention of Jolene McGuff, much to the annoyance of the pastor, who was trying to do the same thing. Jason Controy had his head down and cell phone up, as he trailed behind his parents to their car. Pat finally ceased dispensation of her liquor-fueled platitudes and rejoined me. Jolene appeared unimproved.

I drove us back to Elmcroft in silence. The Controys were ahead of us, and by the time we passed their driveway Jason was already leaping from the car and jogging away from his parents. I frowned as he raced out of sight behind the back of their house rather than step up the front stoop with Kim and David. They pivoted and waved as they heard my truck, and I slowed to offer a salute. Patricia hadn't looked in their direction.

"You want me to drop you off?" I asked Patricia as I hesitated at the bottom of my driveway.

"Oh no, dear, I'd love a little porch time if you wouldn't mind. Sherry's coming over later but I'd rather not be alone today."

"No problem," I said, pulling the truck in. She wasn't frantic, but I knew upset when I saw it. Upset and guilty. Patricia was oozing both.

I brought out two glasses with ice and coke and an old Charleston Gazette from a pile in my living room. We finished off the flask. The deck shaded us from the worst of the heat and I loosened my tie, leaning back in a chair.

"I wish you'd get married, Johnny," Patricia said out of nowhere.

"Well aren't you just the embodiment of society," I said in mock appreciation.

"Oh no, no, not because you *should*," she emphasized, "but because I need a malleable young female nearby. A protégé, you know." She clicked her nails along the arm of her chair. They were classic red today.

I sighed and got back to the newspaper I was attempting to read. I was stuck on an article in the Lifestyle section reporting on the success of Summer Solstice celebrations at a privately owned, clothing-optional resort in the mountains. The liquor made my head swimmy and I kept having to stop and repeat sentences every time my eyes hit the words "nudist" or "Faerie." I flipped up to the print in the corner now and then to ensure I was actually reading the Gazette. That only served for further self-interruption, and the nudists were starting to make me angry. I turned as I heard a car pull up next door.

"Over here, Sherry!" Pat was already trumpeting over the ledge.

A few moments later Sherry appeared at the side steps. Her eyes roved appreciatively around my deck as she paused to lay her hand on a wooden pillar. We exchanged hellos as she glanced at the flask, and then at Pat, and then at me.

"Alright folks," she said brightly, "let's take a walk!"

*   *   *

I trudged behind Sherry and Patricia all the way up and down Talon Creek Road. It wasn't a very long road, but I was sweating liquor halfway through. Somehow Patricia managed to keep up a dialogue with Sherry. The two bounced along with irritating enthusiasm under the searing sun.

"Wish you'd made it, dear, it really was a lovely affair. His little niece got up and sang a hymn all by herself, would you believe," Patricia huffed between power-steps.

"Got caught up volunteering at the suicide prevention hotline again," Sherry explained. It occurred to me there was a lot of excessive action to their movements; I was keeping pace without looking like a circus ringmaster.

"Ah yes. Mondays are the worst, and all that."

"Really, Patricia."

"Well they are, aren't they?"

"Actually Wednesdays are," Sherry said curtly.

"Is that right! Well—oomph." I watched Patricia's head bob as her knee jerked out from under her.

"Goodness Patricia, how much did you drink at that thing? Forget about a walk, let's get you back home. With some coffee." Sherry had taken Pat's elbow.

"No, no, I'm fine would you—there was—" Patricia shook herself free of Sherry and turned pointedly to the hydrangea bush to our left. "I heard something! There's something in there," she insisted, pointing again to the shrubbery lining the Controy's front yard.

Sherry and I went silent, staring into the leaves. I hadn't heard anything.

"I'm sure it's a deer or rabbit or something," Sherry said, taking Patricia's elbow again.

"I swear, Dillon Meers has me frazzled to my last remaining nerve," Pat said, looking a little sullen and allowing herself to be led away. "And," she continued, "my tripping has nothing to do with drink, it's these new heels. Can't do a damn thing in them! I think I'm getting too old for fashion, Sherry. Can you imagine!"

"Oh nonsense, honey," Sherry responded, and their chatter turned to the subject of dinner while the three of us meandered back home.

I marveled at how long Patricia and Sherry must have known each other. You could feel it in the way they talked to each other. There was a velvety smoothness under the surface, no matter what they were saying. I figured that must be the sound of unconditional respect. I wondered how long it took to grow. I couldn't imagine getting there with anyone, much less Patricia. Relationships were temporary; even buildings were temporary. Everything was.

Patricia Murgatroyd had showed up at my front door once. When I opened it she announced 'I think neighborly sugar is just too temporary, don't you? Succulents are forever.' She handed me a little pot with a sprouty green thing in it. 'It's an Aloe plant. Keep it inside. In case you get burned.'

That was the first time I ever met her.

Temporary or not, I remembered stashing that plant in my bathroom and hoping I never met my neighbor again. I hadn't wanted company then. I still didn't, but I relied on her for it all the same. She always knew I needed it. It was easy to confuse pushiness with perceptiveness. That plant had rebelliously thrived in my bathroom.

Patricia and Sherry beat me to my deck as I lingered to stare at the Rhododendron in Meers' front yard. When I caught up, Pat told me to come over for dinner at seven, and the two departed to her place. Left suddenly alone, and having two hours to kill, I wandered inside. I made the rare decision to investigate the contents of my liquor cabinet. A client the year before had gifted me with a single malt Scotch whisky that stared down in subdued tones from the top shelf. I hadn't spent most of a day drinking since I was in college, but there was something rotten in my belly that didn't care. I poured the drink over some ice and took both glass and bottle out to the deck.

For a while I sat, looking out at the woods and sipping. The distinctive buzz of a carpenter bee jarred me back to life. I cast about for the badminton racket; it was leaning against a far wall, glaring back at me. I grabbed it and felt more in control. I whipped the spindly tool around a couple times, practicing. I didn't think killing bees one at a time was very effective, but I needed some palpable change. I swung.

I swung again, and again. In between my swings I drank, gulping down fuel to swing again. Half the time I wasn't aiming for a bee at all; the other half my forceful swings were clumsy misfires. Several times I frantically defended my face from angry bees that had easily missed my attack. I didn't care. I was numb anyway. I took another drink and made it a big one. I wished I were an alcoholic. I wished I had a solid, predictable reason why I did the things I did. But beneath the booze I could feel my rage building. On top of that I felt like a coward. I knew carpenter bees didn't sting. I took a final swing and collapsed in a chair. I no longer cared if the bees ate up every structure in 50 miles.

My phone rang but it took me a couple seconds to distinguish the sound of its ringtone over the buzz in my head. Or had it rung before? I listened distantly as Pat reminded me dinner was ready and Giles was already there and something about Sherry. I said I'd be there in a minute and put the phone down and realized I'd been drinking straight from the bottle for awhile. Or maybe I had just started. I went inside and brushed my teeth, looking at myself in the mirror. I wanted out but couldn't think of a good enough reason. I looked tired. I wanted more to drink. I walked over to Pat's.

Patricia raised an eyebrow when I walked in.

"Sherry can't make it dear, so come on and have a seat, it's ready," she said, balancing a dish in each hand.

Giles was already seated at the small dining table and nodded across to me. I realized I was a third wheel and my head swam. I pushed down the urge to throw up all over the delicate lace tablecloth.

Not even the social stylings of Patricia Murgatroyd saved dinner, which consisted mainly of her apologizing for Sherry not being able to make it, and overcooked pork. I eagerly volunteered to clear the plates when we were all done. On my final trip I lingered for a moment in the kitchen with the room to myself. My whole body relaxed. I could hear Patricia and Giles talking softly through the doorway, and I prepared a statement in my head about needing to leave.

"You've got to be kidding!" Patricia exclaimed as I walked back in.

"Warrant just went out," Giles responded calmly.

"How in the world…" Pat began, but shook her head and reached for her wine glass instead of finishing.

"Well, there was DNA. No fingerprints, but the DNA came back. Sealed the deal."

"So it wasn't…" Patricia trailed off again.

"No ma'am. Nope, it all comes down to the shovel."

I was about to interrupt with excuses for my departure when a frighteningly loud metallic racket burst out from the direction of Patricia's back deck. I jumped and froze, but Detective Giles was up from the table in an instant, drawing his weapon and gliding by me to the back door. He paused for a moment, straining to look out into the darkness. Patricia wordlessly joined him and hovered her hand over the porch light switch. He nodded, and she flicked it on as he yanked the door open.

Jason Controy stood on the deck, halfway stooped in a frozen motion to retrieve a shovel from the concrete floor. He righted himself and shut his gaping mouth. We stared. He cleared his throat.

"Uh. Hi, Ms. Murgatroyd," he said.

TWENTY-TWO

"I just don't know what that boy was thinking," Patricia huffed. She stepped over to the counter to pour herself another drink. I was washing dishes in the sink and Giles was drying. Patricia was having her third glass of wine. I scrubbed mindlessly.

"If he had wanted to borrow the shovel all he had to do was ask," she continued, sipping. "And trying to return it in the middle of the night! And what in the world did he need a shovel for!"

"Kids will be kids," Giles said without humor, wiping a plate with a dish rag. I didn't know how we'd gotten roped into doing the dishes. I guess I had started it, rinsing a glass, and then Giles had stepped up so as not to be the unhelpful guest. Or maybe it was the other way around. There was a perfectly good dishwasher to our left. We were both steadfastly avoiding it.

"Anyway," Pat said, resituating herself on a bar stool and watching us with no small amount of pleasure, "Dillon

Meers is off the hook."

"For the McGuff murder, yes," the detective said. "No usable prints on the shovel, but when the murderer...used it," he paused, "he hit him so hard that he pricked his palms on the fibers of the wooden handle. It was ancient, half rotting apart, left outside too long. And the DNA on the shovel was clear. Only belonged to one person." He shook out the rag. "Zebulon Fix."

"So," I said, pouring out some more soap, "so he—I mean—he was with me. At the ball game. So he murdered Leroy—"

"Not ten minutes before he knocked on your door," Giles said, nodding. "We figure he was the one blackmailing Meers. Remember the note you all found?"

"Oh!" Pat exclaimed from her stool. "What," she addressed our stares, "I had forgotten about the note."

"You always forget about the note," I said.

"He knew Meers had killed his wife," the detective continued, "because he was the one that gave him the false alibi. When Meers went missing, ole' Zeb figured he'd make a better investigator than the police, since he knew the guy pretty well. So he comes over here that afternoon and breaks in. You can see where the police tape was removed from the front door and put back up. And the lock was picked. Mighta thought he knew where Meers hid his cash or something, too. Tried to do it once before, if I'm not mistaken," he said, looking at me, "the day you met him."

"That's right," I said. "And I unwittingly interrupted him before he even got started."

"Exactly," the detective paused and wiped his forearm over his brow. "Anyway, Leroy McGuff, out watering his roses, did see someone across the street that day. But it wasn't Dillon Meers. It was Zebulon Fix exiting Meer's house. The house that was a crime scene. And Zebulon Fix saw Leroy. And had to act fast. He grabbed a shovel from the deck and walked across the street to McGuff, probably leading the way with some yarn about being a worried relative. Zebulon does have a way of being casually charming, when he wants to be."

"Tell me about it," I said, retrieving a suicidal spoon from the garbage disposal.

"They got to chatting, I'd imagine, and Leroy made the mistake of looking down to light a cigarette. There was a lighter and an unlit Marlboro on the ground near him," Giles continued. "And Zebulon Fix struck. One blow to the head with the flat part of the shovel and he was down. Then another for good measure."

"Smoking kills," Patricia said flatly, and I grimaced. "But killing him seems like such an overreaction," she added.

"Not when you had a record like Zebulon Fix. A breaking and entering charge, especially with the intent to steal, would have violated his parole and sent him back to prison for a long, long time. Plus, Leroy McGuff wasn't a dumb man. We don't think he was believing a word of Fix's story. And we think Fix knew it."

"So he murders my neighbor and is suddenly in the mood for baseball?" I asked, trying to wrap my head around things.

"Not quite," Giles said. "He had a problem. Someone else had seen him in the subdivision that day, as he was pulling up the road."

"Oh! Oh! It was me!" Patricia said almost gleefully. "I saw him when I was on my way to—well, on my way out," she amended, glancing at the detective.

Giles narrowed his eyes at her, but continued stacking plates. "Exactly. You saw him. And to be honest, Pat, you might have been in a lot of trouble had you been home."

"Oh my," Patricia said, taking a drink.

"He had to think fast. He needed an alibi. And he knew we wouldn't be able to precisely determine time of death. If he just killed somebody, the last thing anyone would suspect would be for him to then go to a baseball game. And if he took his new buddy, Johnny," Giles glanced in my direction, "he killed two birds with one stone. Coming by to get you explained his presence in the neighborhood."

"God," I said, feeling dirty.

"Yeah," Giles nodded. "He already had two tickets, he was supposed to take his girlfriend. That line to you about her leaving him was a complete lie. We talked to her again after the DNA came back. Once we knew what to push her on, it didn't take long for her to start filling us in on how upset she was that Zeb not only stood her up, but probably 'went to the damn game with some floozie.'"

"Don't take it personally, Johnny dear. You're a terribly handsome floozie." Patricia raised her glass to me, and Giles sighed. I got the feeling he'd committed himself to thinking of me as the coddled, ubiquitous nephew.

"So I was his alibi," I said, ignoring her, and shaking my head.

"You were indeed. We'd assumed all along the murder had happened while you two were at the game. Fact is," Giles turned to look at me, "you drove right past it."

"Holy…" I trailed off, comprehending. I *had* driven right past it. The only reason I had seen Leroy coming home was the hose water that had leaked into the road. On my way out of my driveway that day, Leroy McGuff was already lying dead directly across the street, hidden by his rose bushes. His silly, gaudy rose bushes.

"And there was only one other detail he had to take care of. Before he came to ask you to the game, he jogged aways down the road and flung the shovel away. Didn't have the time or means to clean the blood off it."

"It wasn't that bright," Patricia weighed in.

"Or he was very, very high." Giles suggested. "It was insanity to break into a place in the daytime in the first place."

"I always thought he was kind of crazy," I said.

Patricia sniffed. "Didn't seem to stop you from hanging out with him," she pointed out.

I shrugged. "He was also very charming."

We finished the dishes and Giles walked over to Patricia. "Yes," he said, kissing her on top of the head, "and unlike you, dear, Zebulon Fix is a sociopath every day of the week."

So they were at pet names now. That was fast. I stared at the etching on her now-empty rocks glass and pocketed my phone to leave.

"Oh, you like this one, Johnny?" Pat asked, following my line of sight.

"It's a beaut," I nodded, "Somewhere in the UK?"

"Winchester Cathedral in Hampshire. Drove down from London and spent the day there. You know it's where Saint Swithun was buried. Or rather re-buried." She looked at her cell phone. "Oh! And Saint Swithun's Day is right around the corner, how exciting!"

"Thrilling," I deadpanned.

"It is thrilling," Patricia harrumphed. "It's like the British version of Groundhog's Day."

"It is, huh," I said with a healthy scoop of skepticism.

"Well sort of. Apparently it poured down rain the day they moved his remains, and then kept raining for forty days. Dead men don't like to be disturbed and all that. And so the legend goes, if it rains on July 15, it'll rain for the next forty days. You know, like the groundhog's shadow predicts—"

"Right, right," I said, standing up. "Well, folklore-ish weather predictors aside, I think it's time for me to head back home."

Patricia opened her mouth but Giles stood up immediately, offering a handshake. "Nice to see you again, Jepko," he said.

"Bye dear," Patricia said, somewhat miffed that she wasn't given the chance to invite me to stay for one more nightcap.

I waved a final goodbye as I walked out the back. Behind me, I heard Patricia ask the detective: "And what of Dillon Meers, then? Where is he?"

The porch light was still on from the shovel incident, and I followed its light out to the garden. Every spider in West Virginia contributed webbing in a grand scheme to have me walking like an over-animated zombie all the way home.

*   *   *

Two days later I was driving back from a job site and nearly threw up my lunch. As I pulled into Elmcroft I slowed, trying to process the scene on the road in front of me. Somebody's trash can was upturned on the pavement, and a white plastic bag of refuse was beside it, torn to shreds. Its contents were gutted, scattered across the road by wild animals or wind or God himself.

In the middle of the trash was a horrendously fat groundhog. It was picking through the banquet of debris with humanoid claws. Its massive gut rippled as it nosed around, but as I eased my car forward, it froze.

And then it lifted up on its hind legs and looked at me. I met its beady black eyes. It stayed silent, but I saw its lips curl back, and it bared a pair of long, sharp incisors at me. They were covered with blood. A droplet swelled and trickled off the tip of a tooth, splashing to the pavement.

I couldn't look away. The sky had been darkening, and as I stared, it started to rain. A crack of lightning popped through a nearby tree and finally the groundhog turned tail. He undulated away, disappearing into the underbrush. It began to pour. I shivered, and swallowed, and rolled up my windows.

It was July 15th.

TWENTY-THREE

It rained the next morning. I went outside to work anyway, protected by a stalwart roof and caffeine-numb skin. After several hours my eyes drifted from the laptop screen to the table, and then farther. I looked down, down to the wooden deck floor in need of staining, down through the splinters of wood fibers, down to a crawl space full of hard darkness. My phone rang and I jumped.

"Hello," I said, gulping moist air

"Johnny? Listen, dear, Sherry and I need another Scrabble player, it's just no fun with two, what with the—"

"Be over in a sec," I interrupted. I felt like I could use a drink. Or a distraction.

I scooted my chair out and returned the laptop to the kitchen, then tripped over the cat, righted myself, and was off. I was starting to wear a path from my house to Patricia's, or I guess we both were. The grass didn't care which way we trampled it; it was going to die regardless. I envied the beetles devouring tomatoes in the garden; I was hungry, but I guessed Patricia would have food on hand. I wiped rainy streaks off of my lenses and rapped on her back door.

"Come in!" she called, but I was already pushing the door open.

"How are you, Johnny," a bright-eyed Sherry said from the card table set up in the living room.

"Oh, fine," I said, dragging a wingback across the rug to the table. The chair featured a floral-paisley pattern that almost matched Patricia's dress, but instead clashed horribly. I sat. "How are you?"

"Just wonderful, honey," Sherry said, offering me a clinking bag. "Here, pick some tiles. I'm going to make another pot of tea. You want some?"

"Tea?" I asked, scanning the table. Sure enough, in front of each woman sat a teacup and saucer. The teacups had etchings, of course.

"No thanks," I said, and then turning to Patricia, "They all out of shot glasses in Rome?"

Patricia finally blinked and looked up from her tiles. "What? Oh, Saint Peter's Basilica, yes. Yes. I mean no. Well, I don't know, I liked them." She leaned across the table. "They're the only teacups I have, and some people—" she pointed a not-so-subtle thumb over her shoulder, "—prefer me sober, of all things."

"Hard to imagine," I said flatly.

"Johnny," she said suddenly, eying me, "You're drenched! You didn't bring an umbrella?"

"Couldn't find it," I lied. I'm sure I could have found it, if I'd looked, but it would have taken an hour. It was somewhere in my living room.

"Well, I'll loan you one for your walk back," she said decisively.

"No need, it's starting to clear up." I pointed to the

window, where a lightening sky was giving way to a dull yellow fog.

"I bet we'll have a rainbow!" Sherry said, joining us. She sat a glass of water down in front of me and a plate of buttered toast next to the Scrabble board. "Afraid Pat and I are on a diet," she said morosely, selecting the top piece of bread.

"Tea and toast. I feel like I walked to the wrong house," I said, trying to sound as light as the spread.

Sherry smiled, collecting the teacups and returning to the kitchen.

"Did you say this was Saint Peter's Basilica?" she called back to us.

"Yes, yes, dear, in Rome, you know." Patricia suddenly seemed to have an epiphany She ferociously juggled tiles around on her rack until she sat back with a soft "Aha!"

"We haven't started playing yet," I pointed out, sliding my tiles around unenthusiastically.

"Indeed, my young friend," she grinned as Sherry returned with full teacups.

"Hope you don't mind, we already drew before you got here, honey, Patricia's going first, I'm afraid you pulled an X. She beat my pants off the first round."

"She did, huh," I said, poking a tile.

"Yes, yes. Are we ready?" Patricia was still grinning.

"Go ahead," Sherry said, with a faint frown.

"Eat my…" Patricia grabbed all her tiles and situated them in the middle of the board. "S-A-W-D-U-S-T!"

"Oh, goodness," Sherry said, frown deepening.

"Bingo, bitches," Pat reveled, managing to maintain a raised pinkie as she took a sip of tea. "That's 50 points on top of the 30," she told Sherry, who was scribbling numbers on a small pad.

"I don't like her sober," I said to Sherry.

She looked up. "I spiked her tea with whiskey," she said forlornly.

Pat looked down into her cup. "I thought this was damn good tea," she said, sipping again thoughtfully.

I got up and went to the kitchen, dumping my water and replacing it with ice and whiskey. Two could play at this game. I returned to my seat and pulled my garish chair closer to the table.

"Did you actually go in the Basilica, Pat?" Sherry asked, thumbing her teacup as I struggled to shift tiles into words.

Patricia was pulling new letters from the bag, her bracelets rattling at odds with the clinking of tiles. "Oh yes. Had to see the Pieta, you know."

"Mmm, mother and child," Sherry said, mouth tightening a little. I wondered what she had against children. Or mothers.

"He designed the dome too, you know, of the Basilica. I mean, architecturally, not painted like the Sistine. Did you know that, Johnny?" She bit into a piece of toast and looked at me.

"Hm? Yeah. Yes." I covered a V tile with my index finger, willing it to disappear. It didn't work. The game was making me anxious already, and I hadn't even taken my first turn. I tasted the whiskey. It was smoky and subtle, on par with Pat's usual selection.

"So Giles called earlier. They picked up Zebulon Fix today," Pat said conversationally.

I looked up. "It took them three days to find him?" I asked.

"The girlfriend evidently tipped him that they were looking for him," Patricia explained, as Sherry tsked softly from behind her letters. "They had to stake out a couple places before he finally made the mistake of showing up at one of his usual haunts," she finished.

"So case closed," I said.

"Yes indeed. They even got the confession. He admits to the murder. But would you believe, Johnny—he insists he wasn't blackmailing Meers. Says he didn't make up the alibi. Says he was trying to find Meers, but only because he owed him a lot of money."

"Playing games with them maybe. I guess blackmail would be an added charge?" I asked.

"A felony, I believe," Patricia offered.

"But he admitted to the murder?" Sherry looked up from her letters.

"Yes. But insists Dillon Meers did not kill his wife," Patricia said.

"Misplaced loyalty?" Sherry asked, but didn't sound convinced.

"Weird," I said.

By the time Patricia used the S of my feeble S-I-C-K to spell M-E-R-M-A-I-D-S, her second 7-letter achievement, Sherry and I were already so far behind there was no hope of redemption. We played the game to its excruciating end, squeezing lone vowels into awkward places and doing math on one hand. Sherry absorbed Pat's gloating with good humor; I absorbed it with good whiskey.

Like a spent bar patron, rain clouds finally dried out and left, giving the sun back its view. I twisted in my chair and watched the emerald trees shaking off rain through the window. I had a sudden desire to be anywhere but a living room.

"Hey," I said, "Can I go to the...the place," I detoured, realizing Sherry was there. Did she know about it?

"What are you talking about, Johnny?" Pat asked, scrutinizing me.

"The...in the woods," I pointed out the window, "where we went the other day."

"He's talking about the greenhouse, Patsy," Sherry said, killing my subterfuge.

"Oh! Oh, yes, of course you can, course you can. I might stay put though, afraid all this winning has left me in need of an afternoon nap," she stretched her arms above her head and yawned, as if to prove her point.

"I've heard tea can make you sleepy, too," I said, taking another gulp of whiskey and feeling a little lightheaded.

To my surprise Sherry said: "Can I join you, Johnny? Haven't been out there in a long while."

"Sure," I said to the woman I barely knew. The liquor was making her look more familiar, though.

"You kids have fun," Pat said, returning all the tiles to the bag and closing up the Scrabble set. She yawned again and meandered down a hallway out of sight.

"Would it be a good time to steal all her stuff?" I asked Sherry.

"I'll back the car up. We should be able to fit most of it in the hatchback," she said, nodding. I smiled.

"Let me grab one thing and I'll be ready to go," she said, ducking down the same hallway Pat had taken. She was back in a minute, hefting her large purse over her shoulder.

We headed out the back door, brushing past plants that splattered us with low-velocity raindrops. The air smelled wet, bright and organic, and above us birds were starting to talk again. I led the way into the woods, trying to stay on the path that time had made and time had forgotten. Neither of us talked, and the activity of our movement made the silence palatable.

We got to the greenhouse sooner than I expected; in fact, it took me by surprise, almost like it had the first time.

We rounded a bend and there it was, looming above us out of its camouflage.

As it came into sight Sherry let out a deep sigh. I knew the feeling. How long it had been since Pat brought her out here? Was it the same as our trip? Was this a place of confession for all who came? I felt a little like confessing, and I wondered how much of it was the location, and how much was the alcohol.

We stepped carefully over damp ground and went inside. I walked over to the designated seating area and wiped a finger across the bench. It came up wet. I looked up; the rain had blown through missing panes. I sighed.
Sherry came up behind me and put a gentle hand on my shoulder to move me aside.

"Here we go, honey," she said, pulled a giant beach towel out of her shoulder bag. She used a corner to wipe off most of the moisture, and then laid it out flat on the bench. She sat on one end, patting the other for me to join her.

"Wow," I said, sitting. "You think ahead, huh?"

"My girls used to play softball in school. You get accustomed to rain delays and the aftermath," she smiled.

It was interesting how Sherry played herself down, while Patricia broadcast herself out. They were similar in age; both 60 or close to it, although Pat would never admit such a thing. From what I'd seen, that's where the similarities ended. Patricia clashed where Sherry blended. Sherry's voice was soft and steady, like she'd invented her own brand of sensitive confidence. Her long, dark hair was streaked with gray, and she wore no makeup. Her big, brown eyes looked through our cage of rain-kissed glass and out to the trees. She seemed to know that this was the only way to see a forest from the inside.

"I knew a girl once," I said, and she turned those eyes to me.

TWENTY-FOUR

"Only one?" Sherry asked, smiling.

"Well," I said, "the right one."

"What was she like?" she asked.

"A surreal, slapdash goddess," I said without thinking. I didn't have to think to talk about Darby. "With brown hair," I added.

"Sounds like an adventure," Sherry said.

"Actually she said other people always thought she was depressed. But I never saw it. I still wonder if it was because she was blind around me, or because I was blind around her."

"That's not a question I can answer, honey." Sherry said, taking her gaze off me to look out into the woods again. Sunrays were beginning to jump down from a hundred leafy oculi, and I wondered which one God was peaking through.

"The first time I ever saw her she was breaking into

a private swimming pool on her lunch break "

"Well that doesn't seem very prudent," Sherry said, but a smile was hovering at the corners of her mouth.

"I forgave her," I said, smiling. "She was too alive and too beautiful not to forgive."

"The only sacred things are banjos and beauty queens," Sherry nodded. I thought I'd heard Patricia say that before. I wondered if it was some sort of state motto I was unaware of.

"She was everything that was good in the world, for awhile," I said.

"And now?"

I paused and stared at the petals on one of Patricia's white lady slipper orchids. "She left me," I said.

"I'm sorry to hear that, Johnny."

I sighed. "I never really had her."

"But you two were close?"

"For six months, yes. For an hour or two a day. It was a private sort of relationship. But she was a perfect disaster." I leaned my head back and idly whistled the first few notes of *Sea of Heartbreak*.

Sherry looked at me again. "And someone else's wife?" She didn't say it with any accusation; she just put the question down and let it sit there.

"And someone else's wife," I confirmed, not meeting her gaze.

Sherry rose slowly, putting her hand on my shoulder.

"I'm sure she loved you too, Johnny," she said softly. And then she shouldered her bag and left me sitting in the woods by myself.

When Sherry was out of eyesight and earshot I looked at Pat's orchid again. Darby would have loved it. It was her kind of abstraction, built on microscopic order. There was architecture in nature, I supposed. It was just hard to see. I got up to go home, throwing the beach towel over my shoulder.

The woods seemed to be getting dark and I realized it was already approaching eight. I stepped out into the bright evening of Patricia's back yard and considered going inside to return the towel, but headed for my deck instead. Exhaustion swam around my head, trying to pull my eyelids shut.

I hung the towel over a deck rail to dry, and collapsed into a lounge chair. I looked out and saw Sherry's rainbow. It was low and faint, but it was there. I closed my eyes.

*   *   *

"Johnny? Johnny!"

I peeled my eyes half-open, unsure where I was.

"Wake up, honey," a different, gentler voice said.

I opened my eyes wider now. Two heads floated above me.

"Sherry has something to tell you," Patricia said, clearly now.

I squinted. I was outside, on my deck. On the lounge chair. Where I had apparently slept all night. The sun was glowing from the other direction now, but I could hear soft rain on the roof. I hadn't slept so soundly in weeks. I hadn't slept so soundly in months.

"Sherry has something she needs to tell you," Patricia repeated.

"Let him wake up, Patricia," Sherry said, tugging at Pat's sleeve.

Pat made a harrumph sound and ducked out of sight. A second later I heard the door to my house slide open. Sherry shrunk from view as she retreated to the edge of the deck. I could see the vague outline of the towel I'd left hanging on the rail. It was probably soaked. I closed my eyes again. I got the impression a lot of things had happened while I slept. I didn't much care.

"Here," Patricia's voice permeated my thoughts again, and I blinked a couple times, pulling myself up to a sitting position. She was holding out a coffee mug. I took it and breathed in. My brains were all gummed up from oversleeping. I realized I might be permanently cramped into the shape of the lounge chair.

"Drink," Patricia said. After several moments I took a sip. I could feel the warmth sliding all the way down my throat.

"Sherry needs to tell you something," Patricia said for the third time.

I looked at Sherry. She'd removed the wet towel from the railing and placed it over the back of a deck chair. She walked over now, taking a seat across from me.

"I don't think I've ever told you my full name," she said quietly.

I stared into her face; into the familiar brown eyes that seemed to be pleading with me. And then I knew.

"Sherry is a nickname for Charlene. Charlene Lotts. See, honey, I think you knew my daughter." She swallowed. "I'm Darby's mother."

I was wide awake now.

Nobody ambushed like Patricia Murgatroyd.

*   *   *

The calico cat thudded down off the railing where she'd been napping. The impact reverberated across the deck wood like a miniature earthquake. She swayed over to Patricia, and then Sherry, leaning an arched back into their calves. Then she sat back on her haunches beside Sherry and looked at me, letting out a plaintive, accusatory meow.

"You're...yes. Yes. I knew your daughter." I had about as much control over my words as a pebble in a landslide, and things were sliding fast.

"Sherry came back and talked to me after the greenhouse last night, Johnny," Patricia spoke up now. Her tone was clear and even, like she wanted me to pay attention to every syllable. "We usually don't talk about her daughter. Bad enough I was living right down the road when it happened, poor dear couldn't even stand to visit me for months," she reached over and squeezed Sherry's shoulder, and then went on: "But we talked last night, Johnny. We talked all night. Something you said out at the greenhouse—well, Sherry figured out who you were talking about. We didn't mean to, of course, but we figured it out, you see." She cleared her throat and glanced at Sherry.

"Johnny," Sherry took over, leaning forward to take the coffee cup out of my fingers and wrap her hands around mine, "the police didn't announce it publicly, but Darby was pregnant. Ten weeks pregnant. They did a DNA test on the—the fetus." She paused and blinked. "And. Well, Dillon wasn't the father. That's why—" She squeezed my hands and took a breath. "That's why they reopened the case. That's why they think he killed her. Because he knew she was pregnant with another man's child."

"No. No—no." I shook my head, and kept shaking it. I looked at Patricia. "No," I said again. "That's not—no."

"I don't think he knew either, honey. I don't think so either," Sherry murmured.

I sighed, nodding robotically. She lifted her shoulders and let them drop.

"Johnny?" She asked, bending down to catch my gaze. "Johnny...were you the father? Were you—the man that she used to tell me about? Were you the father of that baby?

And did she...did Darby leave you when she realized she was pregnant?" Sherry's eyes watered now, and Pat had drawn closer, her hand closed firmly on Sherry's shoulder. The rain around us picked up, drumming on the roof, pounding into the ground.

"What? Well...well, yes," I said weakly, trying to will away the clouds in my head. "I was...I was the father," I said a little louder. My gaze had escaped Sherry's and was plastered to the deck floor, but I could hear Pat take in a breath.

Something snapped. I pulled my hands out of Sherry's clasp and stood up abruptly, knocking over the mug she'd set on the floor. The black coffee splashed out across the wood, staining wide before trickling through the cracks. I kicked past the lounge chair and stumbled over to the railing, planting my palms on the ledge land leaning into it heavily. I looked out into the haze and breathed deep, nausea tempering my anger.

The women didn't make a sound behind me. No one moved to clean up the spilled coffee. Even the cat was absent now. But the rain kept falling.

"Johnny," Sherry said once more. I turned around and leaned back against the railing, hands splayed along either side, shoulders shrugged in defeat.

"Did you kill my daughter?" Sherry said. I could hear the bite in her whisper. Patricia turned to her friend, wide-eyed.

I blinked in surprise and looked up.

"No," I said hoarsely. "I killed her husband."

*   *   *

Sherry Lotts gasped. Patricia Murgatroyd slapped a hand to her forehead and steadied herself with the other on an armrest as her whole body collapsed forward. I didn't move. That numb feeling was back.

"What—what do you mean," Sherry choked.

"Oh, God," Patricia whispered beside her.

"You mean it was suicide?" Sherry cried. "She really...she...and you..."

I walked past them into my house. The house that held every piece of paper I'd never thrown away. When I came back out neither of them had moved.

"She left me this," I said, handing the Sherry the thin piece of ruled paper, filled with Darby's scrawly handwriting.

"I thought it was a breakup note," I said. "By the time realized...it was too late."

"You really killed him," Patricia was staring at me with wide eyes. "I thought...I thought you wrote the blackmail note to frame him."

"You knew I made the blackmail note?" I asked curiously. My hands were in my pockets. I stared despondently at the rain with my back to Patricia.

"I came by for something one day and you weren't here and I let myself in, and I...well the magazines...that you'd cut the letters out of, they...well a couple had fallen out of a pile on the floor, and I was trying to put them away, and..." she trailed off.

"I did make it to frame him," I said. "I did everything to frame him, so that everyone would think he'd run. So that no one would think he was dead. Except you almost did anyway, didn't you?" I bit back the frustration in my voice.

"Yes, well, for awhile I did. Very," she swallowed, "very clever having me 'discover' the note, John. Very clever."

"Thank you," I said, turning.

Sherry sat holding Darby's suicide note with shaking

hands, tears streaming down her face. She looked up and I could see concern joining the sadness in her eyes.

"Where is Dillon Meers, Johnny?" she asked through her tears.

I looked down to the deck floor. I looked past the deck floor, to the hard darkness underneath. To the coffin-sized slab of concrete I'd poured before I had the deck built on top of it.

"Underneath us," I said.

TWENTY-FIVE

"I didn't...I didn't plan it," I said, turning my back to them again. Beyond the deck, along the driveway of the empty house next door, was the row of rhododendrons I had stared at for the past four months. They were in bloom at last. The big white flowers had sprung up everywhere, like cotton candy pinheads on giant dark green cushions. I could see why Darby loved them, now.

"I moved here after Darby died," I began. "I don't know why. Some kind of attempt to know her after death. To hang on a little longer. Reinvent myself. But pulling closer to the idea of her just put me in a deeper hell than the one I was already in. And I didn't count on her husband still being around." I glanced at the women behind me. Sherry's head leaned on Pat's shoulder now. Their hands were linked tightly. Patricia rested an elbow on the table, white knuckles grasping the edge.

"I worked construction before I got my architect's license," I continued. "I was all set to pour a little concrete stoop out here with a mixer I'd rented. Made a better tomb instead." I shrugged and stared towards the door and down, at my hidden sepulcher. "Buried his money and credit cards and passport too. I thought..." I wiped condensation from my glasses. "I thought I could make it look like he killed her and ran. I had some bloody gloves, with gunpowder residue. Still sitting in a plastic bag in my truck, from when she got a nosebleed at the gun range one day. That's what they found in his closet. I put it there. I kept one of his credit cards and ordered a taxi to the airport from his house. Pulled a cap over my face and took it there. It's not that long a walk back here from the airport. Only took about an hour.

"I blame myself for her death. I taught her how to use that gun. And I never saw how sad she was. And I blame the world for her death. Because it never loved her enough. But mostly," I stopped as the rain cranked up a notch so I had to almost shout. "Mostly I blamed Dillon Meers. You don't have to pull the trigger yourself to kill someone. He was a bastard. I knew it the first second I laid eyes on him. I knew it from the first words he ever spoke to me." The rain stopped. I turned toward the women.

"He came over here one day, right after I'd moved in. He was wasted. Stunk of beer and weed. He wanted to borrow an axe. Said he needed to chop up some firewood. He was going to have a bonfire. Wanted to get rid of 'a lotta shit his no-good dead wife' had left behind.

"I didn't even hesitate. It was the end of the work day and I'd just slipped my tie off. I grabbed the tie. I grabbed him. It's not easy to strangle someone with a tie." I let out a low chuckle, remembering. "But I managed. Darby had picked out that tie."

I glanced at the women. They were both looking at me with faces of ill-disguised horror. I looked down. My fingers had been working. They had been busy. They were loosening the tie I was wearing, the tie I'd slept in. They were tugging it. Caressing it. I stepped away from the women towards the rail and let my hands drop.

"I did it for her," I said.

"Johnny," Patricia spoke up now, voice cracking. "Your morals are killing you, dear. You can't handle what you've done. You've painted outside your own lines."

"I know," I said.

I looked at Patricia. She was scared and sober. She kept eye contact with me, but her mouth betrayed her, tight-lipped and quivering. Sherry clung to her, but in her eyes was a strength her daughter hadn't had. That I didn't have.

"You need," Sherry choked, "to turn yourself in, Johnny."

Patricia leaned over and picked up her cell phone with glitter-gold nails, then hesitated when it was halfway to her face. She looked at me like she was waiting for permission. She looked at me like she was trying to measure the weight of the world with her eyes. She looked at me like she thought I might kill them, too.

She didn't know I could see the edge of the police cruiser at the bottom of my driveway, peeking out from behind a Rhododendron bloom.

"Don't think twice," I said. "It's alright."

EPILOGUE

Patricia Murgatroyd sat in a lawn chair in her garden, watching. Half a city construction crew crowded around and inside Johnny Jepko's deck. Crime scene tape ringed the railing. The neighborhood had more houses with yellow tape than without, she thought wryly. She reached down and stroked the calico cat as it brushed by.

Supervisory policemen and forensic analysts hovered over a man with a jackhammer. Upended deck planks were scattered all over the place. Half the men were waist-deep in a giant crater in the floor. The jackhammer briefly roared to life, followed by cautionary shouts and garbled instructions. She was mildly perturbed; the crime scene had attracted more people to the deck than her sunset soiree.

A tall figure climbed out of the crowd and started strolling towards her. He removed a pair of dusty plastic goggles as he approached. Silas Giles took a seat in the empty chair beside her and let out a sigh.

"You knew he did it," Patricia said, looking ahead.

"Oh, now," Silas began, "Not till you and Mrs. Lotts

filled us in on his relationship with Darby, really, and—"

"You set me up!" She looked at him now, frowning a little.

"We were going to haul him in anyway, Pat. We just needed to know where the body was. I thought he'd be a little more open with you. People like you, you know."

Patricia harrumphed and clicked a nail on her chair. "You know you had Sherry thinking he murdered her daughter, for goodness sake!"

"Where's your drink?" Silas asked.

"I stopped drinking." She examined the nail.

"You what? Well. What now?"

"I'm going to adopt this cat," she said, nodding towards the calico. They stared at the jackhammer crew for a moment.

"You worried about Johnny?" he asked.

"I'm going to miss him. But structure and confession will be good for him. He needs to be saved from himself."

Patricia looked out over Johnny's deck to the forested mountains beyond. There wasn't a cloud in the sky.

"All this room out here," she said, "and he managed to get himself into a real dead end."

THE CUL-DE-SAC

ABOUT THE AUTHOR

R. L. Young was born and raised in the foothills of Appalachia, embattled by june bugs but burglar free. The author gave up various dreams of hot air balloon aviation and snail racing to pursue writing, and whiles away the days on an old typewriter at the tail end of a cul-de-sac where not a damn soul ever gets murdered.